5/95

From This Day Forward

Book Five
of the Enduring Faith Series

SUSAN FELDHAKE

ZondervanPublishingHouse
Grand Rapids, Michigan

A Division of HarperCollinsPublishers

From This Day Forward
Copyright © 1994 Susan Feldhake

Requests for information should be addressed to:
Zondervan Publishing House
Grand Rapids, MI   49530

ISBN 0-310-47931-2

Cover design by Jody Langley
Illustrations by Bob Sabin
Edited by Anne Severance

Printed in the United States of America

*For all the people worldwide
who are also "friends of Bill's" (and Rozanne's)*

chapter
1

Salt Creek Community
Union Township
Watson, Effingham County, Illinois

"WONDERFUL DINNER, MOLLY," Seth said, pushing his chair back from the head of the long dining room table. "You outdid yourself this time and prepared a regular 'groaning board' for our enjoyment."

"It was marvelous, dear," Seth's aging mother chimed in, giving the young woman a fond, approving smile.

"When it comes to the culinary arts, our Miss Molly's keepin' right up with my Liz," Brad Mathews added, proud of the girl he'd help raise.

"She'd give my Sylvia a run for her money, too," Rory Preston complimented, and slipped his arm around his wife's slim shoulder as she helped Fanny Beth, their small daughter, finish up the food remaining on her plate.

"Yessirree," Brad added, settling back in his chair and cupping his steaming mug of coffee, lightened with fresh cream, "when the time comes, our Miss Molly will set some feller a right fine table."

"Which is more than will be said for me," said Molly's elder sister, Katie Wheeler, with a light laugh, speaking up before anyone could josh Molly and inquire if she had some particular bloke in mind.

Widowed Seth Hyatt added his chuckle to the Salt Creek community's schoolmarm's self-deprecating laugh. "We're all given traits and talents as the good Lord sees fit, and you have many capabilities, Miss Katie. Why, you've only to ask my children . . . or any of your other pupils, for that matter."

Katie set her china cup on its saucer with a muted clink. "Yes . . . I suppose so. But . . ."

In her eldest sister's hesitant response, Molly detected the lingering notes of desire for her own husband, her own home, and her own children gathered around her like olive vines around the table. Only another woman who shared those selfsame longings would recognize them for what they were, Molly thought.

A moment later Molly felt herself flush when she considered Brad's compliment, followed by his remark about some lucky "feller" and suddenly realized how it might be construed by others. Was Brad throwing out a broad hint to Molly's employer, Seth Hyatt? Lord knows Lizzie Mathews was an inveterate matchmaker, so it was only natural that her husband might be inclined to follow suit. Was it so obvious how Molly had come to feel about Seth? And about his darling little children who accepted all the mothering Molly had to give? Was Brad tossing Seth a healthy hint in case he was blind to what was right under his nose?

For a moment Molly froze, afraid that her inner feelings were plain on her face. She desperately wanted to escape the dining room that suddenly seemed too crowded with Seth's kinfolk and close friends, who'd been invited to partake of Sunday dinner following church services earlier that morning.

"I–I'll clear the table," Molly said quickly, her voice unusually thin. "Dessert's ready. Blackberry cobbler coming right up!"

With that, the solidly built girl, dressed in stylish but serviceable garments, fled the room.

"I'll help you, hon," Lizzie offered, following her foster daughter from the room, clutching up plates and used silverware on the way.

Not trusting herself to speak, Molly merely smiled her thanks and quickly disappeared into the adjoining kitchen. Across the doorway hung a heavy curtain, created from a length of upholstery material and put there to keep the stultifying heat of the kitchen from invading the dining room.

Molly went directly to the oak sideboard with Lizzie in her wake. Lizzie placed the china and cutlery into the enamel dishpan with a clatter that did not drown out the buzz of conversation from the adjacent room.

Molly could hear Seth talking with Katie. Their easy banter was a disturbing signal that her older sister had achieved an instinctive rapport with her employer that Molly herself had never quite attained.

"After Molly serves dessert," Seth's voice carried clearly, "we'll take a stroll, Miss Katie, and I can show you the improvements we're making in the new sawmill."

"I thought you had just finished up some important changes," Katie said thoughtfully.

"Right you are," Rory spoke up. "But that brother-in-law of mine is right on top of things. He's seeing to it that timberin' in these parts is the last word, he is."

"And why not?" Brad teased. "He doesn't have a woman to shower with his money and attention. So he lavishes his profits on his business."

"Give him time," Rory said knowingly. "Just give him time. He may be stuck pretty tight to the griddle, but I'm reckoning that there's a woman beneath these very rafters appealing enough to make such an eligible widower gladly trade in his freedom for wedded bliss."

"Rory!" Seth scolded, and in such a tone that Molly knew he must be turning purple as the attention of everyone in the room focused on his marital state.

Molly—and likely Miss Lizzie, too—could all too easily envision Rory's teasing, impudent shrug. "Time will prove if I'm right or wrong," he predicted before letting the subject drop.

The two women worked quietly and efficiently in the stuffy kitchen—Molly scooping generous portions of blackberry cobbler into dessert dishes and Lizzie topping them with mounds of fresh, whipped sweet cream. Without saying so, Molly sensed that they were both thinking the same thing.

"Ready?" Lizzie asked when the last dessert had been dished up.

Molly swallowed hard and forced a carefully indifferent smile that she hoped didn't betray her pounding heart. "Ummm-hmmm," she mumbled.

Hesitantly she pulled back the heavy curtain with her pinched fingertips, and allowed Lizzie to precede her into the dining room, knowing she would encounter more than one knowing look.

"Dessert's served!" Lizzie announced gaily.

There were noises of appreciation, followed by an almost tense silence as Lizzie and Molly served the bowls of cobbler with dispatch.

"Delicious!"

"Ummmm . . . wonderful!"

"As good as Ma used to make!"

And for a while there was no further sound but the scrape of spoon on pottery bowl. Molly ate her cobbler without tasting the sweet and sour dessert. To the onlooker, she seemed a thousand miles away, but in reality she was intensely aware of the people gathered in this home that had welcomed her when Rory Preston, returning to the community of his youth, had arrived in Union Township with his wife and daughter, with plans to send for his widowed brother-in-law, Seth Hyatt, Seth's children, and his aging mother.

When Molly's dish was scraped clean, she edged her chair away from the table. "If you'll excuse me, I'm going to do up the dishes. But y'all feel free to sit back and enjoy your coffee and visit," she murmured. "We don't get together like this nearly enough anymore."

Mary Katharine Wheeler began to rise. "I'll help, Sis," she offered.

"No!" Molly said, more sharply than she'd intended and forced a smile to serve as an antidote. "I–I mean that isn't necessary, Katie. You visit with Seth and the family. You're so busy with your schoolteaching that you don't get to socialize much . . . except with the young'uns in class. Please . . ."

Katie looked puzzled, then acquiesced. "If you're sure . . . ," she agreed reluctantly, her expression a bit mystified and registering a degree of helpless hurt.

Molly managed a radiant smile. "Positive!"

Lizzie boosted herself from her chair near the head of the table. "I'll help ya, darlin'," she said. "Miss Sylvia, you stay right where you are. Fanny Beth's head's a-droopin'. With a full tummy, she'll be noddin' off at any moment. And Mama Hyatt, I expect if you'd retire to your rocker in the corner, you'll have a grandbaby slumberin' on your lap before the grandfather clock chimes half-past-one."

"I 'spect you're right, Lizzie," said the elderly woman, whose home until recently had been in the Great Northwest.

Favoring her arthritic joints, she arose slowly and reposi-tioned herself in the rocker, with Brad's gallant assistance.

"And Brad, you be a dear and hold Seth's son, iffen you would," Lizzie suggested. "With the young'uns accounted for, the adults can let their meals digest and visit a bit as Molly's fine meal is settlin'."

"I think I'd sooner walk the dinner off," Seth said, patting his trim waistline. "Miss Katie . . . do you feel up to strolling out to the sawmill?" he inquired, his tone casual, as if oblivi-ous to the fact that it was an invitation she had been counting on all day.

Katie arose with quick grace. "Certainly. I'm eager to see what you've accomplished. You've not been here long, Mr. Hyatt, but you've certainly done wonderful things for our neighborhood. In fact, for the entire region. We're all indebt-ed to you. Why, your sawmill has provided security for the families of so many of my students."

"Those are kind words indeed, Miss Katie, but I could return the compliment, for people in these parts are willing and conscientious workers. But please . . . call me Seth. I always think of 'Mr. Hyatt' as my late pa." He offered his arm to Mary Katharine and they stepped through the open screen door.

As it banged shut, Molly heard her sister's delighted response. "Then Seth it is," Katie agreed, her tone almost flir-tatious in her pleasure over the small intimacy invited.

With that, Molly escaped into the kitchen, while Lizzie lin-gered long enough to see Mother Hyatt ensconced in the rocker and Brad nestled down on the settee with Seth's son. Rory was seeing to the needs of his young wife, who was in the family way again, and Sylvia shifted about, trying to get comfortable, as she held their dozing child, Fanny Beth. The little girl had been named after Rory's sister, Lizzie, and their late mother, Fanchon Preston, who was still sorely missed following her violent and untimely death years earlier in a freak accident. And that wasn't all that grim season had held for the family. Lizzie's late husband, Jeremiah, had suffered almost mortal wounds from the vicious kick of a maverick mule and, weakened, had succumbed two years later to the influenza.

Molly could not resist a peek out the kitchen window. What she saw wrenched her heart—Seth and her sister walking along the path toward the sawmill, his dark head bent to catch some softspoken comment. So intense was the shaft of pain that rocked her that she feared she might stumble beneath its ugly weight. With the uncomfortable moment suspended in time, Molly struggled to discern the source of the unfamiliar sensations. What were they? Frustration? Loss? Disappointment? Unrequited love? *Jealousy?*

"All these and more," Molly acknowledged in a miserable whisper.

Tears glimmered in her eyes, and a mealy lump lodged in her throat. To add to her trouble was a burden of guilt, for she realized that such unworthy emotions were beneath her as a sincere Christian seeking to live out her commitment.

She poured hot water from the kettle into the dishpan and fanned away the steam that wreathed her head. With the other hand she swiped impatiently at the filmy sheen of moisture and tears.

"What'd ya say, Molly-girl?" Lizzie asked, her tone vibrant as she entered the kitchen, the one room where Lizzie Mathews always felt at home.

"No–nothing," Molly said, blinking quickly.

But Lizzie Mathews, a perceptive woman if ever there was one, as keen and intuitive as her own mother had been, was not fooled. "Goodness, Molly, what's wrong, darlin'?" She laid a compassionate hand on the young woman's shoulder, feeling the tension coiled in the stocky frame.

"Nothing," Molly insisted, quickly pivoting away.

Lizzie's gentle hand turned her right back and she scrutinized the girl who'd been like a daughter to her. "But you're cryin', sweetheart. Somethin' must be troublin' your soul, girl, and you can tell me what it is and I'll share your burden. Why, you Wheeler girls have been like my very own. You know you can trust me. Not a word will pass my lips 'cept to the Good Lord when I tell him all our daily cares 'n' concerns."

"Truly, Lizzie," Molly murmured, drawing in a deep breath and releasing a heavy sigh, "there's nothing the matter. It—it was the steam. It was so hot it just made my eyes water there for a minute."

The older woman wasn't convinced. "Well . . . if you say so."

But as Molly turned away, the ugly emotions bubbled deep within her, feelings she suddenly seemed unable to control. Risking another tormenting glance out the window, she saw the man she loved with her beautiful older sister, obviously the object of his growing affection.

"So that's it, is it?" Lizzie asked gently, coming up behind Molly to peer over her shoulder. Her soft comment was scarcely more than a breathy sigh, and it was Molly's undoing. A sob escaped. There was no condemnation in the comforting hand Lizzie laid on Molly's arm. "You're real attracted to him . . . to Mister Seth . . . ain't ya?"

At the probing question, Molly's face flamed hotter, embarrassed that another was privy to her most private heartache. But she knew she couldn't lie to Miss Lizzie and settled for giving a curt, somewhat defiant nod. "I reckon I am," she admitted on a shuddering sob. "I don't like it, but I can't seem to help myself."

"You poor darlin'," Lizzie said, drawing Molly into her warm embrace. "You love him . . . and he has eyes only for her." She shook her head sadly. "Give it time, Molly-girl, for if it's meant to be, then one day Seth Hyatt will see you different. And then . . ."

"No!" Molly's tone was harsh with determination. "I–I won't wait around, hoping, praying, leading myself on with fond daydreams of what might be . . . when the stark reality is that it'll never happen . . . 'cept maybe at my own sister's expense."

"Don't just give up, Molly," Lizzie said. "I know the man admires you right smart. And his young'uns couldn't love you more if ya'll were blood relations."

"Yes!" Molly hissed, and her eyes, awash with tears, glowed with fiery feeling. "That's true enough, but . . ."

"Shh, child!" Lizzie cautioned. "Someone's bound to hear. Come on outside for a spell." She maneuvered Molly out the back door and onto the stone stoop.

Shielded by a screen of towering maple trees, Molly loosed a storm of emotion. "I know Seth Hyatt 'admires' me . . . just as he would a–a stick of furniture that serves its purpose in his house! I daresay he couldn't hire a better cook or a more devoted nursemaid for his children. And there's even a fair chance he couldn't find a better housekeeper for the fee. But the reason I've served him so faithfully and refused the raises he's offered, is because I've labored out of *love*, while Seth sees it only as a *business arrangement!*" she finished on a wail of pure grief.

"Oh, Molly, I know, I know," Lizzie crooned. "I've seen this comin' for some time now."

"I do what I do to make Seth happy, knowing all the while he's probably thinking of Katie—my beautiful, educated, *slim* sister," Molly choked out the words.

"You may be right," Lizzie agreed reluctantly, unwilling to add to Molly's anguish. "There does seem to be a . . . special spark . . . 'tween the two, don't there?"

Molly could only nod. Somehow, though, with the unvarnished truth out in the open, she felt a little better. "Since the death of Pa and Miss Abby, and with Marissa taking off the way she did . . . or being spirited away by that desperado . . . I have no blood kin but Katie. I love her so much, and I–I won't let a man come between us, or put Seth in the position of having to choose. I–I'd rather drop out now . . . before Katie finds out how I feel." Molly sniffed. "They do make an awfully comely pair, seein' them together."

Lizzie drew her close once more. "What a wise, wise woman you are, darlin'," she comforted, smoothing tangled wisps of shiny chestnut hair from Molly's tear-blotched face. "You're so much like your mama, sweetheart. Sue Ellen Wheeler would be so proud of you. I know *I* am." Lizzie gave the girl one more hug before releasing her, then, as was her nature, got down to the business at hand. "So what're you going to do? It'd be pure torment to stay on."

"There's only one thing to do. I have to leave," Molly murmured, her tone both pained and resolute. "I–I'll tender my resignation to Seth, and soon . . . but not so soon that he can pinpoint the real reason." She paused, marshaling her thoughts. "I'll give Seth my notice, allowing him time to find someone else to fill the position. Then I'll make a new life for myself . . . somewhere else . . . far away, if need be."

"Oh, Molly!" Lizzie gasped.

"Lord willing, I want a man of my own someday, Lizzie,"

Molly said, her normally mellow voice suddenly high and squeaky. "A good, strong, Christian fellow who'll love and want me as much as I want him."

Lizzie was quick to protest. "Yes, but . . . must you talk of goin' far away?"

Molly shrugged, her confusion evident. "Maybe the good Lord is leading me to leave the Salt Creek area so my path can cross his . . . whoever he is . . . and so I won't hunger after a love that isn't meant to be," she added sadly.

Lizzie squinted in thought. "You may be right, Molly-girl. "'Cept for Seth Hyatt, there ain't another eligible bachelor . . . leastways not one I'd pick for you . . . in all o' Union or Watson Townships. But I could ask around . . . maybe in Effingham."

"*No!*" Molly was adamant. "I'm planning on going to Effingham, but I have a feeling it'll only be temporary. I've hankered to apprentice at the millinery shop there. Seems to me a woman alone needs a vocation so she can support herself. And I wouldn't want to be a burden to anyone."

Lizzie smoothed her own coronet where the auburn tresses were shot through with gray. "That's a fine idea, Missy Molly . . . although, if you'll pardon my bluntness, a millinery shop ain't exactly goin' to be the best place to meet menfolk! You'll be more likely to see a gaggle of fussy ol' spinsters, penny-pinchin', hard-to-please married ladies, a bawdy woman or two, and . . . ."

Molly shrugged. "That's not important, Lizzie. The way I figure it, if the Lord has a man in mind for me, our paths will cross, even in the most unlikely spot." Then a frown crumpled her forehead. "I'm not a pretty woman," Molly admitted with a gesture that caused Lizzie to assess the young woman from head to toe. "I know I have a kind face, and I'm

15

probably pleasant enough to look at, but I haven't the kind of beauty that causes menfolk to steal a second glance when they see me on the street. And I haven't a figure as lithe as some might prefer. I've always been a right strong girl, you know, built buxom-like. And then there's my limp." Molly shifted on the stoop to favor her bad leg.

"I know you and Brad did your best, setting my leg when it got broke and the creeks were flooded so it wasn't possible to get me to a doctor. And you'll never know how much I appreciate your tendin' to me. But you know my limp causes some folks to stare, and that's not a flaw a man is apt to over-look."

"Oh, Molly-girl," Lizzie said softly, her expression warm with love and respect, "you've given this a lot o' thought, haven't ya?"

Molly nodded. "Yes, Lizzie, I have. So I'll be leavin' soon for Effingham, and if God wills, perhaps someday to parts unknown."

Lizzie sighed. There didn't seem to be anything left to say. "We'll miss ya, darlin'."

"It's not like I'd be moving far away, never ever to return," Molly reminded her with a weak laugh.

"Well, I can't help dreadin' that day. I'm like a mother hen, wantin' to collect her chicks around her, bein' there to cluck and flutter over 'em and keep 'em all safe in my sight. I promised Pa Wheeler I'd always look out for y'all, ya know."

"I'm not a child anymore, Miss Lizzie. And while I have no plans to go farther than Effingham, I've got to be pre-pared to venture where the Lord leads." Molly gazed out beyond the copse of trees into the distant meadow. "I may not strike out in search of a man, but I can't guarantee that I won't go looking for my twin sister. With Marissa gone, I feel as if a part of me is missing. That's why I can't let a man come between Mary Katharine and me. I've already lost one sister . . . I can't risk losing the other because we love the same man."

"Reckon if anyone can understand that line o' logic, I can, darlin'," Lizzie said. "I remember only too well how heart-sore I was when Rory was away, and I felt I'd drove my little brother off with my own self-righteous judgin'."

A reflective silence sprang between them as the leaves moved overhead, the breeze causing an almost comforting hush.

"I was just thinking, Lizzie, that maybe one of Brad's daughters would be an ideal housekeeper for Seth and his family. What do you think?"

"I think you're right . . . again."

"Good," Molly said, feeling a tiny part of her burden lift. "Now that I've made up my mind, I want to leave soon, but I wouldn't want to cause Seth a problem. Thankfully, his children are fond of your girls, especially Miss Jayne."

"She'd be the very one!" Lizzie agreed, brightening. "If Seth's agreeable, o' course."

"I don't doubt he'll be relieved. And if Mother Hyatt is as kindly disposed toward Jayne as she's always been toward me, the transition will be easy all around."

Lizzie cocked her head, helpless to suppress a rueful grin. "It sounds quite final-like, don't it? Well, whenever you're ready to go, Molly-girl, Brad and I'd like to transport ya to your new home and see to it you're settled in proper."

"You'll be the first to know," Molly promised. Impulsively she moved back into Lizzie's motherly arms, reveling in the older woman's strength and approval, knowing that however far she might roam, there were these waiting arms and a welcoming hearth to greet her upon her return.

"Dishwater's coolin', darlin'," the ever-pragmatic Lizzie reminded her. "Work's a-waitin'. If we hurry, you and Katie might get a chance to visit before Seth hitches up the carriage and takes her back to the teacherage. I expect you've got a lot to tell her."

"That I do!" Molly agreed, feeling unexpectedly buoyant. She was suddenly eager to share with Katie all her own glowing plans for the future and to wish her sister the very best . . . and that included Seth Hyatt, the man Molly had loved and lost.

chapter
2

Chicago, Illinois

THE CLOYING HEAT and humidity clung to Marissa Wheeler like wet wool as she made her way down the dusty city street. She was on her way to join a small knot of people who had gathered to board the streetcar when it arrived.

Marissa fanned her face with her hat, not only for the cooling breeze it produced but to chase away the tenacious flies that swarmed this area of the city not far from the Chicago stockyards. The combined odors that made up the stench of Packingtown reached out to penetrate the very walls of the apartments and homes sheltering the slaughterhouse workers and created a wholly dispiriting atmosphere.

To the casual observer, there was little to betray the fact that this frail, wasted young woman had once glowed with vitality and good health. The thin, one-time country girl's dark hair had lost its silken sheen, and the hard life endured here had already cost Marissa her legendary beauty. It would take more than a cursory glance to see beyond the faded, lifeless eyes, the emaciated figure, the sallow complexion that refused to yield to the artful use of paints and powders.

Although she was still but a lass in years, Marissa Wheeler felt old in spirit . . . old enough to die. And a part of her suspected the truth that if an improvement in her circumstances was not forthcoming before the year was out, she'd have to face a time when body and soul parted company and she breathed her last on this earth.

Instinctively Marissa knew that in her present straits she couldn't survive another Chicago winter. She'd barely made it through the last bitter season before spring had arrived. Even now, with summer bearing down relentlessly, there remained troubling health problems, especially the hacking cough that had so far resisted all her homemade remedies.

Life in Chicago was difficult. There were days when Marissa despaired to the point that she no longer even feared death but felt she would welcome the release found in its embrace. As bad as living was, surely dying could be no worse. And perhaps it would even be an improvement.

While Marissa had moments when she dared hope that the next life would be better, she seriously doubted that she would find paradise. The very blackness of the deeds she had committed in the recent past—some forced on her, others committed of her own free will—seemed to rule out the forgiveness that would afford her so much as a small space next to the coal bin in one of her heavenly Father's mansions in glory.

The truth was, that in the time since she'd departed Effingham County and turned her back on the people who had cared about her, Marissa had broken most of God's laws in outright defiance . . . and mangled the rest, if only through default. Leaving the teachings of her childhood and embracing worldly ones had been difficult at first. Why, even the second infraction had carried with it a weight of guilt. But after that her transgressions had blurred into a stultifying sameness. Her pangs of conscience, she noticed, had begun to diminish as her godless behavior increased.

Marissa had learned how to lie.

She had cheated.

She had stolen.

She had even sold herself—her attractive body and charming manner—all that she had of value in the world. At the time, it had seemed the only option in order that she might keep food in her stomach and life in her body, wrapping herself in a few greenbacks as a hedge against the big city, its fallen nature reflected in the viciousness and depravity of its godless citizens.

She couldn't help wondering if Brad and his boys, along with other men in the neighborhood, had set out to bring her back. Maybe they had . . . and maybe they hadn't.

Perhaps they'd been all too glad to get shed of her, for she had become something of a problem to them, she now realized. At times she'd been plumb hateful to good-hearted Lizzie and kindly, well-meaning Brad, who had taken her and her sisters in when her own folks died. She still stung with shame at the memory of her defiance toward Miss Lizzie, who certainly never deserved such sass.

And Pa, God rest his soul, had not been available to rescue her from her folly this time. She knew he'd have been looking for her if there had been breath in his body. How mortified he would be to see her like this, she thought with a pang of remorse. He'd be so ashamed of her, yet she knew a part of him would be moved to compassion, for she was aware that he'd had a walk on the wild side as a youth. Oh, he'd chastise her, that was for sure, most likely give her a whack on the bustle, adult though she was. For he'd recognize the willful, headstrong child within, challenging all she'd been taught.

A small smile crept to her lips at the memories and her thoughts flowed back to the past. The many times she'd riled Pa to the point of voicing his indignant disapproval had actually been worse than when he'd pinched her ear and propelled her into a corner to "think upon your errant behavior for a while, Missy!"

Molly, her twin, had almost never required a hard word or an act of discipline. Molly had always been as good, sweet, docile, and helpful as Marissa had been obstinate and willful.

Pa, oh Pa . . .

Marissa's heart grew heavier with the weight of reminiscing, and her steps dragged as she approached the trolley stop. Stinging moisture gathered in her eyes as she considered the muddle-mess she'd made of her life in the past few years. If only Pa hadn't died of the smallpox. If only, thanks to poor Miss Abby's infirmities and addlepatedness, they hadn't lost the farm to those disreputable chaps who'd shown no compunction about throwing them out of their own home, bag and baggage, after snookering Miss Abby out of their property.

And to think that she, Marissa Wheeler, had later befriended them, begging them to take her with them when they skedaddled out of the community. No wonder she had found no support remaining for her within the family circle, for that rebellious action had been a wholesale betrayal of everything they held dear.

Many times Marissa had regretted her rash decision to leave the safety of the godly little community. But destiny was a cruel taskmaster, and she'd no sooner set her feet to a foreign path than she realized she was in its possession, with her life no longer in her control. Now escape seemed impossible, even though she wanted out and longed for deliverance.

Although Marissa hadn't been inside the walls of a chapel since she'd left Salt Creek and the little church on the bluff, there were times when her thoughts wandered back to Scripture passages she'd memorized over the years. Once, when she'd been near the red-light district, before she'd begun to lose her looks, she had heard a street preacher on the busy corner, quoting one of those selfsame verses.

Perhaps he wasn't a real pastor, Marissa realized, for she didn't know if he'd studied in a seminary or been ordained. For all she knew, he might have simply been a believer like her pa and other men in the Salt Creek community who'd been moved to preach the gospel and tend to the spiritual needs of their neighbors at times when the circuit rider couldn't get there.

But it was for certain that the man's audience was not comprised of the usual congregation who gathered to hear the Scriptures expounded. Instead, clustered about the clean-cut man, whose words rang with conviction, was a small crowd of bawdy women, with painted faces, knowing eyes, and carmine smiles. They heard him out—even winking and egging him on—as he assured them that, with the Lord, all things could be made new. That the worst of sins could be washed away and the reborn sinner's soul cleaned up as white as snow by the blood of Jesus Christ, the Redeemer who had carried their sins in his own perfect body.

Although Marissa's smile had matched the cynical grin of the woman standing next to her, a stout harlot who reeked of cheap perfume and unpleasant body odors, Marissa's heart was wide open that day to the message she had heard. Suddenly there had stirred within her a deep hungering to believe.

The street preacher had recounted the stories of the Prodigal Son, the woman at the well, and the experiences of Mary Magdalene, who was once an immoral woman herself, but who had become one of the Lord's most devoted friends and followers. In fact, forgiven and spiritually revitalized,

23

Mary had served as a special servant during Christ's earthly ministry, her story having been recorded to inspire some other woman who would live long after she had gone on to her reward. A woman like Marissa. . . . At the memory, she blinked back tears.

Marissa recalled, too, how a year earlier, before the truly hard times had descended upon her, she'd taken action to save herself from the life she now lived. Taking pen in hand, she had written a note of apology to her sister Molly. At that time Marissa still had a source of income—the man who not long afterward had ruthlessly cast her aside, forcing her to learn that life was a precarious affair at best.

Marissa had posted the letter, feeling very much as if she were "throwing her hat through the door first," instead of showing up, unannounced, back home. If she were to be met with rejection, she couldn't bear to encounter it face-to-face.

She'd sent the letter to Molly, knowing that if anyone could be expected to forgive her and reach out to her in her misery, it would be her twin. And kind soul that Molly was, even if the rest of them didn't cotton to the idea, Marissa was pretty sure they'd welcome her back into the fold for Molly's sake, if for no other reason.

After posting the letter, Marissa had begun her vigil. Days had passed. Showing restraint, she hadn't bothered to appear at the window of the post office to inquire about a letter for Miss Marissa Wheeler, in care of General Delivery. That is, until a full two weeks had gone by.

After that, she'd stopped in daily, only to be met with disappointment each time. "You're sure you checked carefully?" Marissa asked when the bespectacled clerk returned to the counter to tell her there was still no letter for a Marissa Wheeler.

"Very carefully, I assure you," he replied. "Sorry . . ."

"All right. I apologize if I seemed to doubt you," Marissa said. "It's just that I've been expecting a letter for a long time. And it's important . . . terribly important . . . at least to me."

The federal employee shrugged. "Each postal patron feels his or her letter is 'terribly important,' Miss. It's our policy to treat all the mail with equal consideration. Uh . . . maybe tomorrow."

Marissa turned away, her bleak expression betraying her outlook. "I thought for sure I'd have had a reply by now. It's—it's just not like them to let such a desperate question go unanswered."

The clerk scratched through his thinning hair and grew reflective, measuring his words. "Pardon my bluntness, Miss," he said at last, "but if I may be so bold as to offer a bit of insight, I've learned that sometimes people have a difficult time setting to paper the thoughts in their minds. If they don't know what to say . . . or quite how to say it—especially if their response might disappoint someone—then they say nothing. Therefore . . . sometimes, ahem—," he pointedly cleared his throat, "no answer . . . *is* an answer, if you get what I mean."

It was an idea Marissa had never considered, and it struck her like a blow. Why hadn't she figured it out for herself? Of course! The folks at home didn't know how to tell her that they didn't want her back. So perhaps they figured that if they ignored her plea, then maybe she'd soon figure out she was no longer welcome, and the family circle, which had been steadily shrinking, would close even further, excluding her forever.

Well, she decided, as a wave of almost unbearable hurt

washed over her, she may be impoverished and without a soul in the world to care what happened to her, but Marissa Wheeler had sufficient pride left not to go where she was not wanted!

The gambling man with whom she'd left Effingham, after the saloon incident that ended in a shoot-out, had ceased wanting her soon after their arrival in Chicago. She suspected that he'd found that good times were costly enough for one, but overly expensive if he picked up the tab for Marissa as well.

But reprehensible man that he was, she really hadn't expected him to slip out of the hotel in the dark of night and leave her to face an irate hotel clerk, who demanded money or service in payment for the outstanding bill.

Lacking funds of her own, Marissa had had no choice but to work out the bill—cleaning rooms, emptying chamber pots, helping in the kitchen, exhausting herself over kettles of boiling linens in the laundry room, performing whatever chores they assigned her around the huge establishment.

Surprisingly, the honest labor had made her feel almost good about herself, and she had believed that perhaps she could earn her own way in the world, after all. But when she'd asked the hotel manager to keep her on permanently, he'd regretfully told her that he couldn't afford to add another salaried staff member and had sent her on her way with some advice about where she might apply for employment.

Marissa had set about the task of finding a job in an optimistic frame of mind but soon despaired of finding anything a decent woman could consent to do. As her prospects dimmed, the suggestions of prospective employers grew bolder and some of them, who appeared to be brothers-under-the-skin to the gambling man who'd left her in such straits, dared mention that she perform for pay what she'd done out of a misguided sense of affectionate gratitude.

But desperate people do desperate things, and no longer believing in a Lord to rescue her, Marissa had set about providing for her needs as best she could. That had been months ago, and although the dreams had died hard, she had been forced to give up fantasies of making a good life for herself in Chicago. Not only that, but no longer did she plan for the day she would return to Salt Creek as a cultured, socially prominent lady they'd be proud to readmit to the family circle.

Once hunger and need had driven her to perform the services of a harlot, Marissa realized that there could be no escape, barring a miracle, and she feared that miracles were in short supply for a wanton woman.

Hearing the clang of the trolley, she was jolted from her reverie. Though almost dead on her feet, she hung back, as was her custom, to allow the ladies of good breeding and the foppish gents, who pretended not to know her in the light of day, to board first.

Wilted from the heat and faint with hunger, having had nothing to eat since the night before, Marissa felt herself waver. Looking up, she saw a handsome young man, who smelled pleasantly of soap, talc, and barber's potions. He touched the elbow of a young woman beside him, assisting her as she mounted the steps of the trolley.

Briefly Marissa wondered if she was the young man's girlfriend, but when she made a disparaging remark, decided that they could only be brother and sister for her to display her irritation so publicly.

Instead of boarding the trolley after his sister, the man turned back and politely gestured to Marissa to precede him.

"May I give you a hand up, Miss?" he inquired, offering her a steadying grip.

Caught off guard, Marissa could only stare, unable to recall when she had been treated with such courtesy, as if she were worthy of respect. The moment seemed frozen in time.

"Hurry up, up there!" bawled someone at the rear of the line. "Quit yer lallygaggin', for pity's sake! We ain't got all day!"

Mesmerized by the young man's clear blue gaze, Marissa murmured, "I–I'd be most appreciative, sir," and managed her most carefree smile in months.

For a moment, more precious than the few coins in her snap purse was the fact that she possessed the handsome man's attention and had received from him a smile meant just for her.

As the trolley lurched ahead, Marissa swayed dizzily, whether from the heat, the illness that had finally overcome her strength, or the heady effect of the gallant man's pleasantries. Finding a seat next to the window, she slumped into it.

The man and his sister were seated a few seats behind her, and although Marissa wanted to turn around and steal another glance, she did not dare. Soon there was no opportunity to do so, for another rider took the empty seat beside her.

He was a huge man, no doubt once as big as her pa had been, but obviously a bloke who worked in Packingtown. Apparently, his employment had eroded his health, leaving him with a large frame but little meat on his bones. Judging from the blood and grime and the gut-wrenching stench of him, he was a fellow who made his living working in the infamous killing pits.

Marissa glanced at him from the corner of her eye, hoping

that if he was vermin-infested, the tiny creatures would not crawl from his clothing onto hers during their ride.

He seemed oblivious to the odors emanating from his person. Perhaps his olfactory nerves had been dulled by constant exposure to the pits. Still, some sitting nearby got up and moved in disgust, while a few others pinched their nostrils together or pressed handkerchiefs over their mouths.

Marissa, feeling faint already, believed that if she tried to move, she would merely collapse onto him. So she settled for turning her face away, burying her nose in the palm of her hand, and holding her breath for as long as possible, gasping in another only when her lungs felt as if they'd burst with the effort.

"Next stop!" the conductor cried.

Even though it wasn't where she'd intended to get off, Marissa really had nowhere else to go, so it didn't matter. She knew only that she must escape the man's nauseating presence before she embarrassed herself by retching in public.

"Excuse me, please," she murmured to the filthy laborer as she attempted to brush past him and into the aisleway. "This is my stop."

The man shifted his bony knees and she bumped against him, then tripped over his blood-sodden brogans, the leather slimy with gore. She lurched forward, lost her balance, grabbed for a steel brace, and missing it, stumbled down the steps as in a drunken haze. The passengers, not anticipating such a spectacle, laughed helplessly.

Landing on the street, Marissa gained her balance, only to lose it again when she stepped on a pebble. She dropped once more, this time retching pitifully.

The world swirled around her and she was enveloped in a wave of unbelievable heat, that quick fever followed by a chill every bit as violent. Then instantly the bright daylight darkened before her eyes, and Marissa realized that she was swooning.

"Let me off! I'm a physician!"

She heard the voice, as if at a great distance, as she struggled to cling to consciousness.

It was followed by the strident cry of a woman. "Oh, Marcus, you idiot! Leave the brazen street chippy where she lies! We'll be late to Mama's garden party, and she'll never forgive you for humiliating her in front of the governor!"

Marcus. So the handsome gentleman's name was Marcus.

And what a kind man he was, too, for handing her up into the trolley, as respectfully as Pa had ever helped Miss Abby. Come to think of it, Marissa thought feverishly, Lester Childers, Lizzie's eldest son, had treated her with that same deference when he'd come to call. But she'd soon outgrown the shy, unsophisticated country boy. This man, however, was anything but a country bumpkin.

Marcus's steely voice was like a whiplash that cleaved the air as he made his way through the crowded trolley, his words carrying through the open window. "And I should never forgive *myself* if I abandoned my solemn oath to relieve sickness and suffering wherever I find it!"

Marcus's sister gave a scornful, trumpeting laugh. "I saw how that cheap wench looked at you, Marc! Perhaps you're very much your father's son after all. Poor Mama confided to me that he had a constitutional weakness when it came to agreeable and willing women."

There was a moment of sizzling silence.

"My father was a just and honorable man, his reputation beyond question. But what is not beyond question, my dear, is that you are very much your neurotic mother's daughter!"

"Just wait until I tell Mama! It's too bad you're of age, Marcus Wellingham, so her lawyers can't protect you—and your inheritance—from yourself. Go ahead, help the floozy! Shower her with your wealth, too, even if Mama and I have to make do!"

"You really should hold your tongue, my dear," Marc said as he was about to hop down. "Surely you're scaring away any matrimonially minded man within a radius of two hundred miles!"

"Men!" came the scalded cry that grew fainter as the trolley clanged away.

"Call an ambulance, my good man," came the now familiar voice through the mist of Marissa's fever-induced state. "I'm a physician licensed in the state of Illinois," Marc explained to a passerby. "And I want this woman taken to the hospital where I'm doing my residency. I'll take responsibility for the poor soul."

Marissa could hear the sound of his brisk stride, making directly for her where she lay in a crumpled heap on the sidewalk. At long last, help was on the way.

The man knelt beside her, the shadow his body cast across her sheltering her from the scorching blaze of the summer sun.

She squinted her eyes open, although it took almost all the strength she could muster. It was well worth the effort, for she felt rewarded to the depths of her being when she beheld his kind and compassionate face.

chapter
3

Effingham, Illinois

STANDING IN THE shadow of the train depot, Molly Wheeler clutched a bulging carpetbag and pushed at her dark chestnut hair that was already wilting around her face in the humid July heat. Impatiently she glanced up the shiny tracks of the Illinois Central railroad bed that stretched as far as the eye could see both north and south, with the Pennsylvania Railroad tracks intersecting the county seat town east and west near the weather-faded depot building.

A few people clustered near Molly, waiting to catch the northbound train with a car or two allocated for passengers and the rest to livestock and freight. And always there were the familiar open cars filled with lumpy black coal from the southern reaches of the Prairie State.

Hesitantly, Molly smiled at the other early arrivals. She felt a lump settle in her throat as she looked around and realized that this might be the last time she'd ever see the central Illinois town that had been home to her for her entire life.

Vowing to think happy thoughts, Molly's spirit brightened momentarily when she recalled the farewell party held in her honor over the weekend in the Salt Creek community. Everyone had been there. Even the weather had cooperated by being sunny and unseasonably mild. Area homemakers had outdone themselves displaying their culinary abilities, and it had been an afternoon of visiting and fellowship followed by a group prayer begun by Brad Mathews. Each member of the close-knit community had joined hands, and as they went around the large circle of believers, individuals had voiced their petitions for Miss Molly's future.

Absently, she stroked her purse where she had placed the contents of the money tree that had been presented to her by members of the community. They who had offered their heartfelt good wishes and the promise of continued prayer, hadn't wanted a mere lack of funds to stand between their beloved Molly and the success she so richly deserved.

The tender farewells had been touching. Lizzie had hugged her and had urged her to be brave and to stay in touch. Others had thronged around, patting her shoulder and offering advice. But it had been hardest of all to say good-bye to her older sister, Mary Katharine, who by now was betrothed to Seth Hyatt.

Looking into Katie's clear eyes, Molly knew that her sister hadn't a clue as to why Molly had moved to town, had never suspected that she worshiped the man that had almost immediately upon Molly's resignation, begun courting the schoolmarm in earnest. Molly knew, too, that Katie was a bit hurt that she was leaving before their autumn wedding, using Minnesota's harsher climate as a viable excuse not to stay for the nuptials.

"Don't stay away long, Molly," Katie whispered as they clasped each other tight. "You and I are the only family we've got, with Marissa gone God knows where!"

"I–I'm sure I'll be back . . . sometime," Molly promised weakly, uncertain what more to say.

"I do wish you could be here for my wedding," Katie said, her tone wistful.

"I do, too. I know it'll be a grand occasion. You're made for each other," Molly admitted. "Why, anyone with eyes to see knows that."

"You think so?" Katie asked. "Your opinion means so much to me, Molly. And you know Seth so well, having lived in the same household with his family. Do you really believe Seth and I are well suited?"

Molly gave her sister a solid hug. "I know so. And if you doubt it, you're only suffering bridal jitters!"

"After Seth and I are married, Molly, I'd love nothing more than for you to be here when I bear his first child." Katie blushed rosily. "Will you?"

Molly gave her sister a long look. "I'll be here. I'll write just as soon as I have an address. And I'll keep you all in my prayers."

"As you will be in ours," Katie whispered.

Now, days later, as Molly waited for the howl signaling the train's imminent arrival, she massaged her fingers, red and sore from clutching the grip of her carpetbag, and mused that after that conversation she'd suddenly felt at ease with Mary Katharine, as if the last invisible barrier between them had been removed.

Molly couldn't help grieving, however, that she wouldn't be present for her big sister's wedding. But she'd made up her mind, and there was no turning back. She was exhausted, true enough, but she was also filled with a heady sensation of anticipation that had increased ever since she'd received a response to the letter of inquiry she'd posted to a certain business so many months before.

Now the moment was at hand, and Molly found herself looking forward to the train trip. It would be a chance to sit back and watch the world flit by as she speculated about her intriguing future.

It had been a long walk from the rooming house uptown, as she had picked her way across the muddy cobbled streets that led to the depot.

The day before had been a poignant experience, too, as Molly had exchanged emotional good-byes with the proprietor of the millinery shop and the other girl who labored in the workroom. Here Molly had helped create the simple bonnets for common folk, as well as the more elaborate fashions for the wealthy matrons married to the central Illinois town's most powerful and influential men.

Looking south, Molly caught a glimpse of a dark plume drifting in the cloudless sky. The hazy wisp boiled upward, thickening, and she realized that it was the telltale sign of the train moving steadily toward them. Just then, above the din of the street sounds as the booming county seat town roused itself to meet the business day, she heard the train's first throaty bellow.

Molly was vaguely aware of the thundering hooves of a team of horses on the street, but some folks were always in a hurry, and she didn't even bother to turn and offer a curious glance as they sped by. Instead of plowing on past the depot, however, the team was reined in and clattered to a halt in front of the clapboard railroad building.

"Yoohoo! Molly-girl, where are you?" Lizzie Mathews cried frantically, leaping from the wagon before Brad could get the conveyance properly hitched.

Molly's heart thudded. A thousand dreaded thoughts came to mind. Lizzie Mathews was not a woman to take on so, especially not in public. What calamity had struck the Salt Creek community?

"Over here, Miss Lizzie!" Molly called, waving, and took a few steps to meet her.

"Thank the Lord we got here in time!" Lizzie gasped, out of breath, and smoothed her flyaway hair from her flushed face. "It was nip 'n' tuck all the way. Brad's been a-whippin' the poor horses unmerciful, intent on reachin' Effingham before your train could leave."

"Whatever for? What's the matter?"

"There's a letter from Marissa, Molly!" Lizzie waved the rumpled envelope as proof. "It was lost in a railroad car! Must've slipped down behind a counter or somethin', and no one found it until now. The RFD mailman delivered it this mornin', 'long with his apologies."

With trembling hands, Molly accepted the envelope that had grown grimy with age but was addressed in Marissa's strong hand. Molly tore it open, saw that in her haste Marissa hadn't affixed a date, then flipped the envelope back over. The postmark was smeared, but she could barely make it out. This letter had been mailed a year ago!

"Dear Molly," her sister wrote,

> I suppose you'll be surprised to hear from me. You've been in my thoughts a lot, you and everyone else. I was a fool to run off like I did. But at this point, there's no sense crying over spilt milk.
>
> But mayhap I can set things straight. Molly, my dear twin, I'd like to come home, if you'll have me back. You've a perfect right to be angry and disgusted. And I'll even sit still if Miss Lizzie laces into me, and I won't backtalk her as much as one syllable! But if you could scrape together a few dollars to hurry my trip home, I'd be much obliged. I'd do the same for you, Molly, so I'm hoping you'll come through for me, since everybody knows of the two of us, you've always been the better person.

I'm hoping and praying I'll hear from you soon. You can write to me in care of General Delivery at the main post office in Chicago.

Until then, I remain your devoted sister, Marissa Wheeler.

"Oh, Lizzie, no!" Molly cried, her face frozen in a mask of tragedy.

"What is it, child?" Lizzie gasped, whisking the two-page letter from Molly's trembling hands. "Is she all right?"

Molly was dazed. "I have no idea, Lizzie. She's asking to come home, wantin' us to help her, and she's waited all this time . . . for a reply that never came."

"Knowin' Marissa Wheeler, as hotheaded 'n' quick to jump to conclusions as her pa, she's sure to have reckoned that no response meant we didn't want her! And pride would prevent 'Rissa from askin' more than once."

"I know," Molly agreed, her mournful words underscored by the train's wail as it approached the crossroads south of town.

"What're we going to do–o–o?" Lizzie fretted, her concerned voice lifting in a helpless moan.

"Well, I'll be going through Chicago," Molly said, drawing up her shoulders in sudden determination. "I hadn't planned on stopping there except long enough to change trains. But things are different now, Lizzie. I'll scour the city and see if I can find Marissa."

Lizzie seemed to wilt with relief, and Molly darted her a look of alarm. The woman had always been so strong, so determined, so competent, always one to lean on. Suddenly Molly saw that Lizzie was growing old and tired, willing to pass on to others the heavy responsibilities she had always willingly shouldered. A lump lodged in Molly's throat as she wondered if she'd ever see dear Lizzie again.

"God be with you, Molly-girl," Lizzie said as she folded her tightly into her embrace, releasing her only when the conductor hopped down, positioned his little step stool and called, "All abooooooooard!"

At that moment, Brad approached, a small, solidly packed canvas bag at his side. "Did you tell Molly what we was bringin' her to make her new place in Minnesota more homelike?"

"Oh, Brad, I clean forgot!" Lizzie gave Molly's valise an assessing look, saw the small carpetbag that doubled as a purse. "Think she can tote it?"

"Tote what?" Molly inquired.

"Well, Brad and I, we was over at Seth's place—the one that used to belong to your pa and mama, Molly—diggin' up some volunteer rose shoots offen the graves. . . ."

Molly felt a larger lump in her throat.

"There's the white rose off Sue Ellen's grave," Lizzie went on. "It's really pretty, in full bloom right now. And this bright red peppery wild rose, it's off your dear pa's restin' place. It's hardy—a lot like your pa was—so I reckon it can take them Minnesota winters. And just at the last minute, we grabbed up a yellow rose from the yard at home. I remember when your pa and my late Jeremiah helped you and Marissa plant it when you was but wee tots."

"Oh, Lizzie . . ." Molly murmured in a tremulous tone.

"It's somethin' to remember your fam'ly by," Lizzie said, "so's you can feel close even when we're all far away."

"You don't know what this means to me," Molly sniffed, throwing herself into the older woman's arms.

"I reckon I do," Lizzie said. "My mama tended such a rose garden with slips taken from her dead kin's graves down in

Kentucky. And I'm tendin' volunteers from them in my own houseyard."

"I'll find a place for them somewhere."

"You let me know where to find you, Molly-girl, 'n' maybe I'll come visit. And when I do, I'll bring you a volunteer off the roses from Mary Katharine's bridal bouquet."

"Maybe I can get a rose start from Katie myself," Molly said. "She'd like me to come for the birthin' of her first child, and I promised her—and myself—that I'd be here."

Their eyes met, exchanging secrets in the way of women. Brad stood nearby, unaware of the volumes they were speaking.

Lizzie couldn't help grinning. "Peace . . . ain't nothin' like it, is there?"

Molly grinned back. "Nothing at all," she said and was surprised to find that she was truly serene about her sister's betrothal to Seth Hyatt. For within her carpetbag was a description of the man she would soon meet and would surely one day come to love.

"All abooooooooard!"

Bravely Molly stepped onto the train, tendered her luggage to the conductor, seated herself by the window, and glanced down where Lizzie stood on the platform with Brad, waving as the train began to roll forward. She was still waving until she was but a speck dwarfed by the depot, disappearing altogether as Molly escaped into the distance.

At that moment, Molly's enthusiasm for the future waned, and she unfolded the letter from her twin, which she'd tucked in beside another letter. She read the two pieces of correspondence again.

In both instances, Molly had reason to suffer trepidation over the future. She was about to go looking for her sister. And she was soon due to meet with the man destined to be her husband, knowing that she was not the woman chosen for him by God but selected by the marriage brokers who specialized in transacting the placement and purchase of mail-order brides.

Molly didn't know whether she would be able to locate her wayward sister, and if she did, what condition she would find Marissa in. But even more frightening was the fact that she didn't know what kind of man she had agreed to marry. In his acceptance letter, there had been a terse note, rather rude and written in a rough hand, Molly thought, for a man who was the timber boss of a logging company. But then she'd had only Seth Hyatt for comparison, and Seth was both educated and refined. Perhaps not all timber bosses were endowed with the same traits.

Alas, there had not even been a photo to help her recognize the man she was scheduled to wed soon after her arrival in the town that was only a few years old. Williams, Minnesota, in Lake of the Woods County, was located just a few miles from the Canadian border. Molly shivered in anticipation and not a little fear. It was this unfamiliar country through which she would travel on the way to her new home where she would stake her own claim to hope and happiness.

chapter
4

Chicago, Illinois

MARISSA SENSED A presence in the room. As if being drawn from the deep, she moved steadily toward consciousness, ready to break the surface between a state of not knowing and knowing.

At that instant, her eyes flickered open and she blinked in bewilderment as she took in the room around her—neutral walls, snowy linens, spare steel furniture, an antiseptic odor. This must be an infirmary!

Taking inventory of her senses, Marissa wiggled her toes, her legs, her arms. Everything was intact. No bandages swathed her limbs. Nor were there any apparent cuts or abrasions on her face or other exposed flesh. There remained only that overwhelming sense of exhaustion.

"Hello, sleepyhead. Awake at last?" A husky, apple-cheeked nurse in a voluminous uniform and huge apron greeted her. "We were wondering when you'd rejoin the land of the living."

"Where am I?" Marissa asked, and her voice was rusty from disuse, and her dry lips threatened to crack with the effort of speaking.

"In a hospital," came the perfunctory reply.

"But . . . where?"

"Chicago, hon. Don't you remember anything?"

"No . . . no . . . oh!" Suddenly it came spiraling back. All of it.

Marissa was caught up in a kaleidoscope of conflicting emotions. The hopelessness of her fallen state. The gnawing ache of hunger and illness. Then . . . the longing to see the young physician—her savior—whose intervention had brought her to this safe haven rather than leaving her to die in the gutter of a busy thoroughfare.

"Doctor Wellingham will be glad you're alert again. All the patients love him, claim he's got a wonderful bedside manner. And that he does. But in your case . . . well, he seems to have taken a special interest." The nurse cocked her head appraisingly.

"Dr. Wellingham?" Marissa murmured, her memory hazy. When she tried to think with more clarity, the very effort seemed only to leave her more exhausted, perilously close to swooning again.

"Marcus Wellingham, M.D. Surely you know him, Miss. As attentive as he's been, I assumed you were a friend of the family, although I'll admit I *had* wondered."

The woman's words trailed off, and though she said no more, the spiraling silence expressed what went unspoken. That it was clear that Dr. Marcus Wellingham was a person of position and power in this city, while Marissa Wheeler was anything *but*!

His clothing had obviously come from the finest haberdasheries, his discreet jewelry from stores on streets not frequented by the common man. And his articulate speech, while sometimes expressing impatience, dismay, and even actual disdain for his sister, was, nevertheless, cultured and refined. No doubt Dr. Wellingham was . . . high society.

Marissa pried her eyes open to look down upon herself as

she lay on the crisp hospital bed. She was clean and cool now, but when Dr. Wellingham had happened upon her, she had been sweaty, grimy, wilted, and her dress, worn thin at the contact points, wasn't as clean as she had kept her clothing at home.

And her underthings! Marissa felt herself flush at the memory as she realized that hospital personnel had already seen a secret source of her shame. Her chemise was dingy from sweat and the inability to launder the garment frequently enough. And her drawers! Patches upon patches were all that held them together. And maintaining her one pair of hose so she might warm her legs come winter meant that she had gone bare-legged all summer. How humiliating!

"Never mind what I thought," the nurse spoke again, jerking Marissa from her private musings. "Your relationship with young Dr. Wellingham is none of my concern. What counts, Miss Doe, is that you're better now, and soon you'll be well enough . . . "

"*Miss Doe?*" Marissa cried. Obviously they had her confused with someone else. And if her records were in error, then what had they been treating her for?

"That's what we've been calling you, dear, since no one knew your name."

Marissa was even further confused, until she realized that she hadn't carried so much as a scrap of paper that would attest to her identity. And if she had been as sick as the nurse had indicated, she had been in no condition to answer their questions.

There was so much to absorb that Marissa was left awhirl after the chatty nurse finished her duties in the sickroom and departed for another area of the ward. Assured by the nurse that Dr. Wellingham would be making his evening rounds soon, Marissa anxiously awaited his arrival.

So the kindly young doctor who'd so taken her eye hadn't *been but a marvelous dream while she was delirious with a fever*, Marissa thought. He was a flesh-and-blood hero. To know that he'd taken a special interest in her case caused a sweet rapture, almost painful in its intensity, to blossom within her heart.

Hours later, it seemed, she heard the doctor's step coming up the stairwell at the far end of the hall and proceeding down the marble corridor toward her room.

"So you're awake," he said, pausing at the threshold as if reluctant to invade her private sanctuary.

"Y–yes . . . I am."

Marissa gave him a nervous smile, and rushed to close the conversational gap that had sprung up between them after this initial exchange. "How long have I been here?"

Dr. Wellingham frowned as he examined the charts he was carrying. "Not quite a fortnight."

"Heavens!" Marissa gasped, thinking of the huge bill that would surely be levied for her care.

"Well, you're much, much better, I can see," said the doctor, studying her flushed face, "though you were a very sick girl when I found you."

Marissa nodded. "I hadn't felt . . . well . . . in a long time."

Dr. Wellingham gave her a searching look, as if trying to reconcile several things that didn't quite jibe. "You shouldn't have let your health go like that."

Marissa stared out the window. "I had little choice," she whispered. "But . . . but I feel ever so much stronger now."

"You'll soon be as good as new," Dr. Wellingham assured her. Removing a stethoscope from his pocket, he perched on

46

the edge of the hospital bed to listen to Marissa's lungs after softly ordering her to breathe deeply.

"An–and *am* I . . . as good as new, I mean?" Marissa inquired when he put his physician's tools back into the black bag nearby.

He nodded. "You should be able to go home in a few days. You were carrying no personal papers, so if you'll kindly notify us of your next of kin, we can make arrangements for them to take you home where you can receive the care you need while you're recovering from your illness."

Marissa turned her face to the wall and blinked rapidly to stem a rising tide of tears. She had nowhere to go and, if forced to provide for her own needs in her present state, she wouldn't live to see the dawning of a new year.

Perceiving her distress, the doctor was quick to respond. "My dear young woman, what's wrong?"

She did not answer him right away but wavered between telling him some version of the truth and an outright lie. Then, deciding that nothing was to be gained from delay, she plunged in. "I have no home to go to . . . and no one to care."

The young doctor seemed shocked. "Surely you jest."

Marissa gave a wry smile and shook her head. "I–I'm afraid not," she said breathily. "I–I seem to have been abandoned by my kinfolk. I wrote to them, asking to be allowed to return home, but I received no answer. And, as you know," she drew in a quick, deep breath for courage as she quoted the postal employee, "'sometimes no answer at all is an answer.'"

"But you'll need care, Miss . . ."

"Wheeler. Marissa Wheeler."

"Well, Miss Wheeler, the fact remains that you'll need

proper care," he repeated, "and if you don't receive it, you run the grave risk of having a relapse, a potentially fatal one. I'm not sure you're constitutionally strong enough to fight your way back a second time. In fact, I'm not sure what gave you the strength to battle through this siege. Prayerful intervention, it would appear, for as a man of medicine there were many moments when I'll admit I feared for your life. Surely there's someone you can turn to." He examined her critically.

Marissa shrugged. "No one." She looked away, unwilling to meet his steady gaze, for she knew what had given her the strength to fight the disease that had almost snuffed the life from her body. In addition to the prayers that were doubtless offered on her behalf by these total strangers, there had been her desire to see *him* again, to read in his eyes the kindness and compassion that told her she was a decent human being, worthy of living.

"It'll be several days before we're ready to release you, Miss Wheeler, and I'll see what we . . . I . . . can come up with in the meantime. I'm not a miracle-worker, although I know One who is . . . and I do have an idea. You seem to be an agreeable girl, and despite the illness, a sturdy and capable individual. I might just be able to situate you where you'd receive proper care, and when you were physically able, be allowed to offer your services to repay the debt."

At the moment, anything was preferable to Chicago's cruel streets! "Oh . . . that would be so very kind of you," Marissa whispered, tears of relief moistening her eyes. "Do you really think there's a chance I could find such a position?"

Dr. Wellingham laid his hand over hers. "A very good chance," he said with a smile. *I'll ask Mother for dinner tonight,* he thought. *Surely she can't . . . won't . . . refuse my request.*

Molly was agape when the train neared the outskirts of Chicago the following day, after whistle-stops at countless small towns as they progressed north. The tired travelers were preparing to disembark when she saw the Windy City sprawling out ahead, hugging the southwestern shores of Lake Michigan. Houses and large buildings occupied the landscape for as far as the eye could see in any direction.

A small-town girl, Molly had been to Watson and Effingham many times, but she'd never ventured beyond those rural boundaries to the west and north. She'd only *heard* of the sights to be seen in St. Louis and Chicago, never dreaming how big those cities would be compared to the bucolic villages of downstate Illinois.

Life in Effingham was slow-paced and cordial, with people warmly greeting one another on the street, knowing that even if they hadn't met personally, chances were good they shared mutual acquaintances. In Effingham, Molly never hesitated to ask for assistance, for it was always cheerfully given.

She quickly found that this was not the case in Chicago. The first people she inquired of eyed her with distrust, and only when they conferred with each other in a strange, foreign tongue did she realize they hadn't understood a word she'd said.

Deciding against checking her luggage, Molly trudged along, her limp growing more pronounced as she made her way on the scorching sidewalks in the humid heat. She was wilted and more than a little frustrated before she found the main post office building in downtown Chicago. And she prayed that a postal employee would remember her sister and could give her an address where she could find Marissa without further delay.

"Help you, Miss?" asked the window clerk in a tired tone. "Got something to send off?"

"I have nothing to post," Molly explained, "only an inquiry to make. I'm looking for my sister. I received this letter yesterday morning." She produced the rumpled envelope from her carpetbag. "It was accidentally mislaid in a postal railroad car and was only recently forwarded to me. In it, my sister said I could write to her in care of General Delivery at this post office."

"Hmmmm . . ." the clerk murmured, frowning as Molly passed Marissa's letter across.

"I was hoping that even though some months have passed, someone would remember her."

"I'm rather new on the job, Miss," the clerk said. He glanced over his shoulder, obviously scanning the area for a specific individual. "Excuse me. Let me locate another clerk. Perhaps he can help you."

The young counter clerk disappeared and a moment later returned with an older man. Molly was relieved to realize that the man to whom she'd already spoken had sketched in her plight so she needn't repeat her story.

"Marissa Wheeler, you say?" The second clerk scratched his head, his expression reflective. "Seems like I do recall the girl. Young. Pretty. Acted kinda frightened, if memory serves. She come in every day there for quite a spell. Got so's I hated to admit to her she had no mail. To be frank, Miss, it was sort of a relief for me when her visits dropped off. Then, one day, she just up and quit comin' around a'tall. Figured she'd moved on."

"That's possible," Molly agreed. "Or maybe she just gave up."

"I'm sorry, Miss. Don't know what else to say. It's heart-breakin' what a lost letter can do to folks sometimes. But those things happen. We handle a large amount of mail in a day's time, most of it delivered right on time, too. But there are exceptions, sad to say."

"I appreciate your help, sir, and your honesty." Molly turned away, feeling more tired and defeated than she could ever remember.

"Good luck in finding your sister, Miss. She didn't leave a forwarding order with us, but there are other places you could look for a written record—hotel registers, hospitals, the police station. Even . . ." he paused as if loathe to suggest it, "the morgue."

At the idea, Molly flinched. "I'll do what I can," she said stoically. "But this is a huge city, and I don't have much time before I must be on my way again."

That evening a weary Molly took a room in an inexpensive but neat family-owned hotel. After explaining her sad plight to the sympathetic desk clerk, Molly stowed her belongings in her small, sparsely furnished quarters and then returned to the desk. There the man, with the help of his wife, had compiled a listing of area hospitals for Molly. It was a grim beginning to her search.

But the next day, Molly began to visit hospital after hospital, biding her time until the administrator could sanction some harried secretary to mine the charts in the myriad filing cabinets for a reference to one Marissa Wheeler.

Each time Molly entered a hospital, she felt a surge of hope that this would be the institution where she would find news of Marissa. And each time she left, none the wiser for her trouble. Feeling burdened by the weight of the world, she limped along, finding it harder with each step to muster the courage to go on. And only when she had visited the last hospital on her list did she realize that she had no will to continue the fruitless search.

She simply could not face the round of police precincts, followed by hotels and flophouses where, heaven forbid, Marissa might yet turn up. And if all else failed, the only avenue left to her would be the morgue.

Besides, she could be wasting precious time searching in vain. The last months she and her twin had been together, Molly had detected a wild restlessness in Marissa. She'd lit out of Effingham County with no more roots than a feather, content to be wafted to wherever a whimsical wind might blow her.

According to the few facts they'd learned, a man, little more than a rank stranger, had inveigled Marissa to cast her lot with his and seek adventure in Chicago. But what if Marissa had not tarried there much longer than it'd taken her to write the letter, and without bothering to say a word to anyone, had breezed out of Chicago as quickly as she'd sailed in? Why, by this time, she could be lost within the bowels of New York City or living as far west as San Francisco!

And what if Molly *never* knew Marissa's whereabouts? Why, wouldn't that be easier to bear than learning that her sister had departed this life? As difficult as it had been, lying awake nights, pondering all the fanciful possibilities of Marissa's fate, the very worst would be to know for a certainty that the once beautiful, vivacious, and intelligent girl had breathed her last in some Chicago gutter, her final resting place a potter's field.

This way, Molly thought, she could hold on to hope for the morrow, believing that each new day would bring her closer to a reunion with her twin. With so little to cling to, so little of her own, this bright hope was a possession she would not willingly forfeit.

Molly slept as one who had died that night, her physical body exhausted, her mind too numb to think further.

The next day dawned gray and gloomy, the hotel room shadowy with morning's faint light. Molly squinted through the darkness, satisfied that she had packed her few possessions. And by the time she had wrestled them down the stairs and presented herself at the front desk, she was already exhausted.

"Figure up my bill, please," she asked the clerk.

"You're leaving us, Miss Wheeler? We've enjoyed your stay, the missus and I."

It had seemed like a godsend, Molly had thought, when she'd discovered that the proprietors were God-fearing believers who welcomed her as a sister in Christ, serving her as if by doing so they were accommodating him. "And I've found your hospitality a blessing and a boon. But I must be off to Minnesota. I'm to be married soon, and I shan't be late for such an important occasion."

The clerk beamed with good cheer. "Well . . . congratulations! And I hope you and the mister have a long and happy life, with many healthy children to bring up in the nurture and admonition of the Lord."

"Thank you," Molly murmured, her smile fading at the thought of the unknown future awaiting her in the northland.

She'd always dreamed that one day she would marry for love. Well, perhaps love was for others—for believers who found favor with the Lord or for the heroines of the Penny Dreadful novels Marissa had so loved to read. But for a stocky, plain girl like herself, Molly decided, it was time to travel on, time to attend to the business of marrying . . . if not for love, then for companionship. At least, she comforted herself, she would no longer be so terribly alone.

chapter
5

As soon as the hotel doors opening onto the busy boulevard closed behind Molly, she was overwhelmingly alone once more. The hotel proprietor and his family had been almost like family to her for the past few days, united in faith as they were. Upon leaving them, however, Molly knew that there was no human being within miles and miles who truly cared if she lived or died.

Ever mindful that her resources must be safeguarded against harder times, Molly decided to walk to the train station in order to save the trolley fare. But as her weak leg quickly grew unsteady, and her shoulders began to ache with the burden of her baggage—the clunky valise, the heavy carpetbag, and the canvas tote containing the rose shoots Lizzie and Brad had given her—she succumbed to the temptation to hail a passing hansom cab.

With a smile the driver halted his carriage horse, hopped down to offer Molly a hand up into his conveyance, and settled her luggage in after her. "Where to?" he called back after he took up the reins again.

"The train station," panted Molly, trying to catch her breath.

"We'll be there in record time!" The driver snapped a quirt over the sorrel gelding's hindquarters, and the horse trotted smartly ahead, head bobbing, tail arched high.

On the street, they passed rag pickers, peddlers, street

urchins, and transients. These the driver scarcely acknowledged, Molly noticed, but he tipped his hat to matrons and
their children along the way, no doubt knowing from which
sector would come future paying customers to assure his own
livelihood.

"Here you go, little lady!" the man said, reining in his
horse at last and setting the brake on the carriage. He jumped
down to help Molly from the cushioned seat. Then, with a
grunt, he hefted her luggage and plunked it down on the
sidewalk.

Molly fished in her carpetbag for Pa's leather coin purse.
"How much do I owe you?"

The figure named by the driver was shockingly high, Molly
thought. But when she considered it the price she'd been
willing to pay to keep the family rose garden so it could
bloom in her new life, it seemed a bargain, after all.

Molly tendered a shiny coin.

The man palmed it, then stared down in silence.

Suddenly recalling that she'd once read in one of Marissa's
novels that it was customary to offer a gratuity in some
instances, Molly explored the worn coin case and fingered
out a few more coppers. "And here's a bit of something for
your pocket, to reimburse you for your trouble, sir," she said.
"Please accept it, along with my thanks."

"Why, I'm much obliged, Miss!" the driver responded
happily, his expression brightening. "Now you have a fine
day, you hear? Need a hand with those bags? They're awfully
heavy."

"No thank you. I think I can manage," Molly said quickly,
fearing that she would be further beholden to the fellow. As it
was, she would have to economize on her lunch that day and
perhaps the evening meal, too.

Upon entering the cavernous train station, Molly surmised that it must be rush hour, for so many people were bustling in every direction. They all seemed to know just where they were going and were in a hurry to get there.

Molly, riddled with uncertainty, felt as if she were bobbing in a sea of humanity, as the tide of bodies changed, those streaming from rail cars merging with those attempting to board the coaches soon scheduled to depart for distant destinations.

"Please . . . can you help me?" Molly inquired for the third time, hoping that she wouldn't be ignored again. "I can't locate my train."

She had been studying the chalked messages on the blackboard, hastily and sometimes almost illegibly scrawled information, with a maze of arrival and departure times and gate information.

"Where you going?" snorted a well-dressed man, barely containing his impatience to be off about his own business.

"Minneapolis-St. Paul, sir."

He hesitated a moment. "You'll want to go to the Twin Cities by way of Milwaukee, Miss."

"Oh. I–I suppose you're right. Thank you."

The man, sensing Molly's inexperience, seemed to take pity on her. He quickly produced a gold pocketwatch and snapped open the ornate, protective top case to consult the timepiece. "And you're well advised to hurry a bit, my good woman, for it's minutes away from departure if my memory serves me correctly," he warned.

"Oh, heavens!" cried Molly. "Where do I go?"

"The gate's over there," the man said, gesturing in a direction that, to Molly, seemed frighteningly vague.

Alarmed, her pulse quickened as she clutched her belongings and proceeded at an impossibly brisk pace to the gate where a line of passengers was boarding a coach with a Pullman car directly behind it. Pain ricocheted up Molly's weakened limb as she pressed her endurance to the limit.

The conductor looked around, then apparently not noticing Molly in his haste, hopped down to retrieve his little step stool.

Realizing that he was about to signal the engineer before he swung up into the car, Molly let out a breathless bleat. Then, when he paused to see who had hailed him, she explained in a rush of words where she needed to go and was relieved to learn that she was in the right place and in the nick of time.

The uniformed conductor punched her ticket and assisted her onto the first riser leading into the coach. Molly struggled a few paces down the aisle and fell into the first vacant seat.

A scant moment later the train gave a loud, snapping jolt, grated ahead, and slowly gathered momentum as the steel wheels spun faster and faster over the iron rails. Feeling safe at last, Molly relaxed and settled back to enjoy her ride.

She was feeling drowsy when they pulled into Milwaukee the next day after they'd halted at every whistle-stop along the line to accept or disgorge the railroad's clientele. They would lay over in this city for two hours, long enough for Molly to freshen up and get a bite to eat before she took her seat again and prepared for the longer, and she feared, even more arduous trip across the Badger State, Wisconsin.

Molly consulted her timepiece and realized that it was later than she'd have believed, gauging the time of day by the natural light remaining. Of course, the farther north she traveled, she realized, the longer the late summer days would seem.

After another departure in the early evening light, which soon gave way to dusk, she discovered that Wisconsin was a verdant land of pine forests and hilly, rolling meadows criss-crossed by meandering creeks and rivers. Already she was see-ing evidence of the dairy-based economy, for black-and-white cows dotted the pasturelands.

Soon, as darkness draped itself over the landscape like a vel-vet curtain, and stars twinkled with cold, silvery brightness in the inky night, she could no longer see the terrain through which they were passing.

Then, yawning, Molly felt her head drop forward. Using her satchel as a pillow, she drifted off to sleep, neglecting her evening prayer time with the Lord that was her custom.

Molly was unaware of how long she had slept, but judging from the crick in her neck when she awoke, it must have been hours and hours. The gray veil was lifting, and the canopy of sky was tinged shell-pink as the morning sun prepared to arise from behind the train that progressed steadily westward. Occasionally, the train would screech to a stop in front of sleeping depots, steel clashing against steel, as silent travelers, numb with fatigue, stepped out onto the platform.

Molly felt a sudden sense of buoyancy as she realized that each mile that had rolled beneath the train's wheels while she slept was bringing her that much closer to her future hus-band. Smoothing her hair as best she could and ignoring the rumbling of her empty stomach, she sat up to enjoy the sur-roundings unfolding around her.

Here the land was even more hilly. Now and then craggy outcroppings of rock created interesting formations. Even-tually, the locomotive chugged onto a long railroad trestle spanning a river gorge, and Molly's heart lodged in her throat. It seemed so high, so narrow, and so far down to the riverbed below! Looking down from this vaulted position, she held her breath as the engine strained to crest the steep hilltop. And when the lumbering locomotive succeeded, Molly exhaled in a long sigh.

By the time they were midway across the state, scheduled for a rest stop of approximately an hour, Molly had grown complacent, satisfied that the train would be able to conquer the terrain, no matter how steep and treacherous it appeared.

Thus, feeling confident and relaxed, Molly began to chat with some of the other passengers whom she had met during breakfast in the dining car. So it took her by surprise when the locomotive, attempting another climb, lurched, lost power, and not being able to regain its momentum, began to clatter backward down the steep grade.

All conversation stopped, and the passengers looked at one another in alarm as the train rolled faster and faster, out of control, until it eventually spent itself, coming to a listless halt in the basin of the same broad valley they had left only minutes before.

"What's wrong?" they asked among themselves as the train rolled to a standstill. The air in the lower elevation was stifling.

"Engine problems, I'd wager," said a man seated near Molly, and he settled down in his seat as if expecting a long wait.

"Oh, I hope not!" murmured a mother with two small, feisty children.

"Here comes the conductor . . . maybe he'll have an explanation," said another.

When the uniformed man reached them, his gait was still rolling, even though the train was stock still. "There's a little problem with the locomotive," he explained, "but rest assured the crew's working on it. With any luck, we'll be on our way anytime now."

"I certainly hope so," fretted the mother of two. "My husband is meeting us in St. Paul, and the children are already tired."

"And I have an important business meeting," complained a man in a stiff collar and suit. "First thing tomorrow morning. It'll cost me plenty if I'm a no-show!"

"How disappointing," clucked an elderly woman. "I'd looked forward to being with my daughter and her family before the day was over."

Molly listened to these tales of woe, thinking that she herself might suffer more than mere inconvenience. Stopping in Chicago to search for her sister had necessitated a new schedule that would allow for only two hours between her arrival in Minneapolis-St. Paul and her switch to a different train departing for the harbor city of Duluth. Now, Molly feared, a delay could mean that she would miss her connection altogether.

When an hour passed, Molly's heart sank along with the other passengers who saw their plans falling apart. The train crew, the conductor told them, was working diligently, but the repairs required resources beyond their means.

An air of desolation set in after word was passed that a crew member had started hiking along the railbed in search of a crew on a handcar to speed the news. Failing that, he would have to go on to the next depot so that the agent could telegraph ahead for a replacement. Then the engine would have to be unhooked, hauled to a siding, and the new engine linked to the other cars of the stalled train.

It did nothing for the spirits of the stranded travelers when a man shared his experiences of a train trip West. That misfortune had cost him a full day while a replacement locomotive was dispatched to them.

Hours dragged by. To pacify the patrons, the conductor assured them that the railroad company would find a way to give them satisfaction when they arrived at their destination, whatever the hour of the day. If they were in time to get another connection out, the railroad would pull strings to help them board, and if not, they'd be put up in a nearby hotel, at the railroad's expense, so they could rest up from their trying experience.

It was almost a full twenty-four hours later before the train finally pulled into the station in Minneapolis-St. Paul. Molly and the other passengers were near exhaustion from the rigors of their trip. Several passengers, however, seemed to experience instantaneous rejuvenation when they were able to proceed with their journey within the hour.

Molly, however, was not among the lucky ones. She faced a long night alone in the Twin Cities. Though she had counted on the railroad company's financing her lodging, nothing was said when she left the train. Unable to afford the cost of sleeping quarters, she decided, instead, to spend the night in the station's waiting area. Surely it could be no worse hardship than she had already endured for the past day and a half.

It was only when she was feeling weary enough to fall asleep in spite of the activity around her that her bedtime habit of prayer came back to her. Molly was shaken when she realized that despite the fearsome trials of the trip, she hadn't thought once of turning the situation over to the Lord, no more than a rank unbeliever! How could she have forgotten that everything was within his control, that he always turned evil to good, and that whatever delays she had experienced must be because he had ordained them in order that his divine plan would be played out?

With the realization, Molly was overwhelmed with a strange, unidentifiable sensation, which she decided was an awareness of just how weak is the human will. On the heels of that emotion was another one, a deeper understanding of what her twin must have experienced when she'd entered the big city, been surrounded by worldly people, and found her faith eroding bit by bit as each day passed.

That musn't happen to her! Molly vowed that she would remain on guard, that she would wrap herself in the Lord's protection, seek his direction, and ask for his blessings in her life.

But could she? Would she? When she had already put her feet to a path, one that would lead to a new life as a mail-order bride, with her mate selected by office workers, instead of chosen for her by the One who had created them both?

"Thy will be done." Molly murmured, and hoped that her prayers would be answered, every one, most especially her fervent petition that her betrothed would be not only a fine man, and kind but a Christian gentleman as well.

Chicago, Illinois

"Marc . . . are you sure I look presentable?" Marissa asked, her expression poignant and beseeching.

"You look . . . absolutely glowing."

Not knowing whether he was replying as a physician or as a man, Marissa crossed to the mirror and stared into the shiny tin surface in order to reach her own diagnosis.

Her eyes widened with relief as she scrutinized her features. Although her hair was still not as healthy and glossy as it had once been, still it was clean, pleasantly scented, and styled as carefully as she was able. Her eyes, too, looked brighter, clearer, with a hint of the old sparkle that had been hers before she'd fallen into a lifestyle that had robbed her of her beauty. And although she was still pale, a rose translucence had crept back into her cheeks.

But surely folks wouldn't expect someone who had been ill for a month to be the picture of health. Still, better to have taken on this pallor in the hospital than behind the walls of the Women's Prison!

Marissa shuddered at the thought and then found herself darting a heartfelt prayer of gratitude heavenward. The Lord had spared her what she surely had had coming.

For so long now it had been increasingly easy, even downright comfortable, though, to put the Lord and his will out of her mind in order that what remained of her conscience might prick her less frequently. But with Marc living out his Christian convictions—saving her life and paying her bill— her own stunted faith had been stirred, and she realized that this was one more thing they had in common, diverse as their lives and family backgrounds were.

But to look at her now, in her fine clothes, one might never guess that she was but a poor country girl, while Marc had been born with the proverbial "silver spoon in his mouth," as Pa used to say.

Ah, the clothes, Marissa thought, leaning back a bit so as to capture more of her reflection in the tiny tin mirror. The clothes had made all the difference in the world in her appearance. Not knowing what to purchase for her, Marc had asked Delores, the apple-cheeked day nurse to accompany him to the mercantile on her day off. Delores had made the selections, and Dr. Wellingham had paid for the purchases to provide Marissa with fitting garments to wear upon her release from the hospital.

Smoothing the rich fabric of her stylish frock, Marissa knew that, to look at her now, no one would ever dream that the dedicated physician, soon to complete his residency and establish his own practice, had literally plucked her from the gutter a month before. Once, in conversation, he'd made a reference to "Pygmalion," and Marissa, believing he was referring to the raising of a sow, had felt rebuked until Marc had explained that he was talking about a well-known play. And when she had heard the story, she had been thrilled that he thought her worthy of transformation, while realizing that his remark also drove home the point that they had been born worlds apart.

"Ready to go, Miss Wheeler?" Marc asked, stepping into her room.

"Oh . . . Marc! Yes! But oh, I'm so *nervous*!"

The handsome physician frowned and lifted a restraining hand. "Not 'Marc,' Marissa. At least not while others are around, my sweet. Remember? It must be 'Doctor' or 'Dr. Wellingham.' I've told you what Mother's like. We must be very careful. Right now we can't let her know that my interest in you is much more than that of an attending physician for a patient."

Marissa, who'd felt so confident a moment before, was drenched with cold dread. "Marc . . . I mean, Dr. Wellingham . . . your mother's going to hate me, isn't she? She's going to recognize me for exactly what I am . . . was . . . and . . ."

Marc looked surprised and not entirely pleased with the directness of her question. He looked away, unwilling to meet her gaze. But he quickly recovered. "Of course not, silly girl. She's going to like you just fine. Because we're going to see to it that she and Sis have good reason to adore you, just as I do."

Marissa studied him. "Do you *really*?"

"Yes, really."

Marissa was dumbfounded. "But, Marc, it's so *soon*. We've only known each other for a few weeks. What will people say? What will they think? When they realize . . ."

"Quite frankly, my dear," he interrupted her, "it's none of their business, so long as the Lord and I know what is in my heart . . . and yours."

Marissa looked up at Marc, then down at herself and gave a feeble, disparaging gesture. "But why me, Marc? You could have your pick of women. Wealthy debutantes. Girls with power and prestige. Why *me*?" She felt duty-bound to confront him with his curious choice even as her pulse quickened with delight at the prospect that Dr. Marcus Wellingham could be hers.

"Why?" Marc looked thoughtful for a moment. "Well, initially, I was drawn to you out of a sense of compassion, pure and simple. Poor soul that you were, I knew you'd die in the street before the next day's dawning if I left you to your pitiful plight. I knew, too, that you'd surely die if carted off to some hospital ward and left to the largesse of society. So, in a spirit of charity, I decided to involve myself in overseeing your welfare."

"Oh . . ." Marissa murmured, unable to stem the disappointment that stole into her mind at the unromantic truth.

Marc noticed and playfully chucked her chin. "Then, after you were cleaned up and lost that ghastly pallor, I must say I was captivated by your charm, my dear. All the staffers on the ward remarked about the beautiful young woman they found beneath the layers of grime."

She blushed, recalling how they had seemingly paid more attention to her toilette than she believed the average patient was afforded. "They were very kind."

Marc nodded. "And as I got to know you, your lovely qualities, your character, convinced me that we were actually very compatible. That's when I realized that I had come to care about you far more than I've ever cared for any woman before."

Marissa studied his earnest face and was relieved, for she sensed that while Marc wouldn't actually lie to her, although out of deference for her feelings, he might word unpleasant news as gently as possible to soften the blow. But she clung to his words—*compassion, charity . . . care* and *compatibility*—and realized that they spoke of a solid and maturing relationship.

"Positive, dear girl," Marc went on. "I've convinced Mother that you're from a respectable family . . . that you're hard-working, industrious, and highly gifted and talented."

"Now I *know* she's going to despise me," Marissa moaned. "I'll never be able to live up to such a glowing recommendation."

"She knows everything wonderful that there is to know about you, Marissa," Marc insisted. "I've told her all there is to tell . . . well, that is, *almost* everything."

Marissa was instantly alert. "And what is that?"

Marc flexed a muscle in his jaw. "To be perfectly truthful, my dear, I . . . ummm . . . withheld from her how much I care for you, Marissa. Mother doesn't know that I . . . that I . . . feel I've fallen in love with you."

"Marc!" Marissa gasped in a whisper, as pleasurable sensations enveloped her from head to toe. But her euphoria was short-lived.

"And, trust me, darling girl," he said in a grave voice, "it's important that Mother not find out just yet. She'd be very piqued, I'm sure. As controlling and manipulative as she is, I'm sure she has no intention of letting me do something so rash as choose for myself the woman I will marry."

Marissa's heart sank. No doubt Mrs. Wellingham had a lengthy list of families with marriageable daughters—accomplished and wealthy debutantes—whom the society woman felt would be a suitable matrimonial match for her very eligible bachelor son.

"I know, Marc . . . I mean, Dr. Wellingham. I can appreciate how careful we must be, especially since I'll be established in your home as a housekeeper. It certainly wouldn't do for others to think we were attracted to one another . . . personally. And I have nowhere else to go."

He nodded, relieved. "It's best to present the situation as a professional arrangement, and nothing more. I'm glad you understand."

"I do." Marissa managed a game smile, even though her heart felt as if it would burst if she couldn't shout from the street corners that she was in love with the most wonderful man in the world! And that he, the finest gentleman who ever walked, cared deeply about her, too!

"Good girl," Marc said softly, laying his hand on Marissa's smooth cheek. "But I promise you, the day will come when I'll declare my love for you to one and all. However, until the time is right, we must wait . . ." his tone grew ominous, "or risk inciting forces who would conspire against us."

"Marc . . . what do you mean? It scares me when you say things like that."

"Trust me, Marissa, there are things you'd be happier . . .

and safer . . . not knowing. But have faith that someday the time will be right."

He drew Marissa into his arms. She nestled her head on his chest, content to hear the solid beat of his loving, compassionate heart. She gazed up at him with helpless adoration. "For you, Dr. Wellingham, I could wait forever."

"I'm not a patient man, Marissa. And I pray I won't have to wait forever to make you mine before God and man."

At the implication, Marissa's breath caught. She felt a swell of joy unlike anything she'd ever known singing sweetly in her veins, making her feel more alive than she'd ever felt before. "Oh, Dr. Wellingham," she sighed, unable to contain her delight.

"My Marissa," he murmured. "Just one kiss before we go."

Closing the hospital door with his heel, Marc captured her more securely in his embrace, groaning softly as their lips met first in fiery need, then clung in bittersweet hope, not knowing just when they'd be able to share such a moment of intimacy again.

"Soon, Marissa, darling, pray that it will be soon. My medical education will be completed, I'll be ready to begin my practice, claim my rightful inheritance, and take you as my wife . . . going far, far away if we must."

Marissa laid her hand on his cheek. He turned to drop one last kiss into her palm, now soft again, where a month earlier it had been leathery, lined, and grimy.

"I would follow you to the ends of the earth," Marissa whispered. "Where you go, I will go."

"Until then, I shall live for that day . . . and night . . . when I possess you as my treasured wife."

chapter

6

Minneapolis-St. Paul, Minnesota

IT WAS WITH a sense of great relief that Molly finally boarded the train bound for Duluth, minutes before noon the following day.

Once seated in the coach, her natural optimism prevailed once again, and she clasped her hands in her lap and closed her eyes, the better to focus on a prayer of thanksgiving and ask for guidance as she faced her new future.

Once they'd left the environs of the city behind, Molly was lulled by the gently rolling hills that swept out of the Mississippi River Valley. The countryside was like scenes she'd seen in a stereopticon—clear blue lakes, fringed with green, snowy seagulls hovering overhead, their wings tipped darkly with gray and black feathers. An occasional white-tailed deer could be seen grazing at the edge of thick pine forests, the trees growing so close together that if a man entered the timber, Molly suspected he would be swallowed up within minutes.

It was a lush and rugged land but strangely calming in its wild, untamed beauty.

As they progressed northward, Molly realized that they were nearing the famous Mesabi Iron Range, centered in the area that had been called "The Arrowhead Country," and she felt a poignant tugging at her heart, a gentle homesickness for

71

the mother she had never known. Sue Ellen Stone, Molly's ma who'd died giving her birth, had once lived in this land as a young bride. At the time she had been married to mining boss, Nate Stone, Jeremiah's father, who'd died of pneumonia the winter before the young widow and her young son had ventured to Illinois. They had left with little more than the clothes on their backs, faith in their hearts, and a deed for property found among Nathan's possessions, the fulfillment of a debt paid by an employee of the mining company.

For the thousandth time, Molly wished she'd had a chance to get to know her mother. Others had told the Wheeler girls of Sue Ellen's Christian charity and sweet disposition, and some had even likened Molly to her mother, while comparing Marissa to the girls' pa, Alton Wheeler, once a rogue and a gambling man, as unlikely a husband for the godly woman as could be found.

Molly's smile deepened as she remembered Pa's words, actually seemed to hear the inflection of his voice echoing through the caverns of her mind as he told Molly, Marissa, and Mary Katharine the amusing story of how he and their mother had met. And over the years, Molly had never been able to travel along Banker Street in Effingham without looking almost reverently upon the spot where Pa claimed that he, while under the influence of demon rum, had nearly run Sue Ellen down with his team of Clydesdales.

The petite widow, dressed all in black, had been standing at the side of the street, intent on hailing a passing teamster, when Doc and Dan, then in their prime, had roared into town, nearly trampling her underfoot. At that moment, from his perch on a steamer trunk, Jem had been woolgathering, wondering how he and his mother could possibly make it the rest of the way to the property on Salt Creek, still ten miles away. So engrossed was he in his thoughts that he had looked up at the last minute to see the tiny woman disappear in a cloud of dust, apparently beneath the hooves of a team of wild horses.

But, to the immense relief of both Jem and the driver, she had suffered nothing more than a powerful fright. And to make up for the way he'd stormed at the innocent woman, in his gratitude that she had been spared any serious harm, Alton had felt beholden to see her and her young son safely to their new home.

Ah, it had only seemed like a chance meeting, Pa had said, for he had soon come to believe that the moment had been planned for him and Sue Ellen since before the foundation of the world. For in her he had found his heart's resting place.

Oh, could it be, Molly hoped, with an almost aching sensation in her chest, that even though she'd made a hasty decision to become a mail-order bride, the Lord might bless her, too? That she might find the love of her life?

"Havin' fond memories of home, young lady?" asked a grizzled old gent sitting across the aisle.

Momentarily confused as she was jolted from the past, Molly stared at him, then shook her head. "Why, no, not really," she responded politely.

"Beg pardon for bein' so bold," he went on, "but I saw the bittersweet smiles playin' across your face, and I was struck with the thought that it was the expression of a young lady about to go home to familiar landmarks."

"Actually, I've never been to these parts before," Molly confessed, "although my mama hailed from around here. But she left over two decades ago."

"Ah, then you must be goin' to visit relatives."

"No," Molly said. "My kinpeople are all in central Illinois, down around Effingham . . . east of St. Louis."

The old man's expression brightened. "Recollect that I was through there once upon a time. It's a purty fur piece downstate from Chicago, ain't it?"

"Yes . . . yes, it is!" Molly exclaimed, amazed to find someone who knew about Effingham this far from home.

"Right nice town, too," the man continued. "But a heap different from what we're seein' now."

Molly nodded in agreement.

"So what'll be your final destination, if you don't mind my askin'?"

By now, Molly was feeling right at home with the stranger. "Williams. Williams, Minnesota."

"Don't believe I've ever heard tell of the place."

"It's a new town," she explained. "A lumbering town. It's only a few years old, as I understand it."

"Ah . . . and there's many a boom town in the northwoods, Miss. Some'll be here ten years from now . . . only bigger and better." He shrugged. "And some won't last a year, leastways not once the lumberjacks cut and move out the harvestable timber, leavin' ghost towns and a sorry mess of treetops and ravagement behind."

"You've traveled these parts?"

"That I have, Miss," he said. "Put in my share o' time in the woods, loggin' before I got hurt, cookin' for the crew after I was well enough to be up and around. But the life of a 'jack is a bitter lot. And winters are harsh. I've opted for warmer climes, myself."

Molly was curious. "Just what is that region like around Williams?"

"Ain't sure, exactly, though I might be able to give you at

74

least a sketchy idea iffen you could tell me some of the bigger towns around."

"Baudette to the east, and . . . just a moment." Molly retrieved the letter in her satchel. Consulting it, she replied, "Warroad on the west."

The man gave a brisk nod. "Beautiful country, that. I worked for the Meloney Brother timber outfit, and we logged a-plenty in those parts, cuttin' logs all over the northern part o' the state."

"Really!"

Squinting in reflection, the man spoke on. "It's thick with tall stands o' timber—Norway pine, Jack pine, spruce, tamarack. Birch and poplar and balmies, too, not that they're worth much, 'ceptin' for pulpwood."

"Is it a pleasant area?"

The man shrugged. "Ain't very developed, that I can tell you. I 'spect that there town ain't nothing more'n a water tower along the railroad sidin', a lumber office, a hotel, a church—if they be God-fearin' folk—and either a mercantile or a company store. Likely little else, 'ceptin' maybe a saloon or two. Seems lumberjacks can't live long without their . . . uh . . . diversions."

Molly felt a sudden chill. Why, she wasn't sure, but she'd expected to find her new home on a par with Effingham at best, or Watson at worst, and she felt a little unnerved with the dawning suspicion that Williams, Minnesota truly was "God's forgotten acreage," as the old fellow had called it.

Her sense of unease increased after a few more probing questions that revealed far more than she had wanted to hear, and Molly began to fear that she might be making the mistake of her life. For if the man she was to wed didn't like her looks, or if she changed her mind about *him*, she didn't know how she would make her way, for surely there was no call for stylish bonnets out here in this wilderness. And it was doubtful that she had sufficient funds to take her to a better place.

The conversation with the one-time lumberjack, who now traveled around the country supporting himself as a jack-of-all-trades, made the trip from Minneapolis to Duluth pass quickly. But Molly fell silent when, from a high bluff, she was able to see the harbor area of Lake Superior. The city of Duluth seemed to crawl up the steep hillsides. Houses jutted from the most unlikely spots as streets and avenues—carving routes from the banks of the great lake to the uplands—created almost sheer drops.

When they arrived at the train depot, the elderly fellow shook her hand. "Well, my best to you, ma'am."

"And the same to you. I've enjoyed meeting someone who's familiar with the area with which will be my new home."

"Take good care of that luggage, Miss," the old fellow warned, nodding toward her valise. "Where you're goin', you won't be able to purchase no more weddin' finery."

"Yes, thank you . . ." Molly's voice trailed off as she was suddenly struck with a new concern. And the elderly man had disappeared before Molly could admit, even to herself, that she hadn't packed a trousseau. That there was no wedding gown.

She had planned, instead, to make one just as soon as she arrived in Williams. As well as she could sew, she knew she could complete a suitable wedding garment within a matter of a few days.

But what she hadn't reckoned on was that the kind of fabric she needed would not be available in Williams. Not at any price. And having have done without so much already—forfeiting a courtship, eschewing romance, abandoning all ideas of true love—Molly couldn't deny herself a proper wedding gown, too, one befitting a bride who was marrying the right man for all the right reasons.

But dear God, what if she was marrying the wrong man . . . and for all the wrong reasons? It was a possibility that Molly dared not entertain. So, instead, she focused on her immediate need—a wedding dress.

The train that was to take her north to Grand Portage, in the United States and then cross over into Canada, was due to leave within the hour. But Molly wouldn't be on it. She couldn't be. For despite her obvious limitations—indeed, because of them—she was determined to go to her new husband as beautiful a bride as it was possible for her to become. And even with the delays along the way, one further postponement was necessary if Molly was to make her prospective husband proud when they exchanged their vows.

She simply had no choice but to stay overnight in Duluth in order to go to a fabric shop, select yard goods suitable for a wedding gown, spools of thread, cards of buttons, and ready-made lace, since she hadn't the time to tat her own. Plus a veil. She *must* have a veil. Surely in Duluth one could find fine netting that would allow her to create a headpiece worthy of the loveliest bride in the state of Minnesota.

Unable to bear the idea of one more night spent catnapping in a public place, Molly walked to the nearest hotel, registered at the desk, and left her belongings in the comparatively sumptuous quarters. Then she treated herself to a fine meal in the hotel dining room before inquiring at the desk for the addresses of fabric shops within walking distance.

The helpful clerk jotted down the names and street locations on a scrap of foolscap and slid it across the marble-topped counter. "There you go, Miss!"

"Thank you very kindly," said Molly. "And may I trouble you to send someone to knock on my door at six in the morning? I'm dreadfully tired, and I fear I'll oversleep and miss the afternoon train to Grand Portage."

"I'll make a note of it right away, Miss Wheeler. Six A.M." he said, applying the ink to an area in the register. "Have a pleasant stay, and we hope you rest well."

"After the fine dinner I just enjoyed, I think I'll surely sleep like a babe," she said as she turned away and limped toward the staircase leading to her second-floor room.

Molly took a warm bath, shampooed her hair and brushed it dry, then slipped between the clean, crisp linens that smelled of fresh air and sunshine. Adjusting the feather pillow only once, she said her prayers and snuggled beneath the comforter. She was fast asleep almost before she had closed her eyes.

Although Molly had allowed several hours for her shopping expedition the next morning, she was relieved to find what she was looking for when she entered the first establishment.

The price was a bit more than she'd planned on spending, but realizing that she might shop the city over and still not find anything better, she followed her best instincts and told the shop girl how many yards she wished to acquire.

"I'll need some thread, too," Molly said. "And some lace."

The girl took the bolt of material over to another area of the large store and matched the thread to the fabric. Finding some lovely lace within her price range, Molly asked her to cut some yardage and wrap it up, too.

"And I'll need some material for a veil," she added.

"Oh, this is to be your wedding gown?" the clerk asked, her eyes brightening.

Molly nodded shyly. "Yes."

"You lucky girl!" the clerk whispered. "You'll make a lovely bride." She lowered her voice and confessed, "I'm hoping my beau will soon ask Papa for my hand."

"Then I hope so, too," Molly said sweetly.

"My best wishes to you and the lucky bridegroom," the clerk called after Molly as she left the store with her purchases. "And good luck to you and your young man."

On the way back to the hotel, Molly basked in the warm sunshine of the balmy day, realizing that she was beginning to feel almost like a real bride, not a mail-order matrimonial match. This must be what Katie was experiencing as she made her plans to wed her beloved Seth. Once again Molly felt a pang of nostalgia that neither sister would be present to share the other's wedding day, to hear the sacred vows exchanged—*"to love, honor, and obey, from this day forward. . . ."*

Her head was awhirl when she retrieved her luggage, checked out of the hotel, and arrived at the depot, allowing herself plenty of time to catch the afternoon train for Grand Portage.

The two-hundred-mile trip to the city located on the border between the United States and Canada was more grueling and exhausting than Molly had expected. More time-consuming, also, for the train stopped at almost every small town along the route that snugged close to the rim of the northwest shore of Lake Superior.

As they crossed the Rainy River at Grand Portage where the French Voyageurs had had to shoulder their gigantic canoes and portage from one waterway to another, the train paused for an extended stop at the depot in order to clear customs.

Hard wooden benches lined the perimeter of the drafty waiting room. Here, for the first time, Molly was able to peruse a map of Ontario, flyspecked and faded with age and tacked to the wall. She was dismayed to discover how much of the trip still lay before her. She had known that Williams was just a few miles past the Canadian border. But what she had not discerned from the information presented her by the marriage broker, nor the letter from her intended, nor from railroad-line officials, was what difficult connections were necessary to reach the tiny lumbering town.

Her heart sank when she studied the map. The route she was to take progressed steadily to the northeast to Thunder Bay, the first settlement of any size. There she would have a layover before she could catch a westbound train that would take her on to Aitkokan, midway between Fort Frances and Thunder Bay.

Fort Frances was located centrally between Aitkokan and the town of Rainy River, Ontario, on a boundary water tributary of the same name, where the Canadian National Railroad line crossed over into the United States, entering the U.S.A. at Baudette, Minnesota. From there it looked to be a twenty-mile trip until the train would grind to a halt at Williams, her final destination.

Studying the rail map again, she saw that the train would remain in United States territory for another thirty miles before it crossed the border again. It could take *days*, and Molly wondered if she should telegraph ahead to let her intended know of her newly scheduled arrival.

Reluctant to spend unnecessary funds and feeling sure her bridegroom-to-be would understand her plight once she had a chance to explain, she convinced herself to save her story for the time when they would meet face-to-face.

By the time Molly had spent four more days on the Canadian National Railroad train, she was vapid with exhaustion and her confidence in what she was doing had all but disappeared. Her spirits lifted a bit, however, when the freight train, pulling the passenger train in which she was riding, halted at Baudette to clear customs as they entered the United States and she realized that the end of her journey was in sight.

Initially, when Molly had received correspondence from the marriage brokerage firm in Chicago, she'd entertained visions of a quick trip to northern Minnesota, never dreaming it would be so draining. She'd also daydreamed about meeting the man who was about to become her husband. She'd pictured herself, looking her very best, alighting from the train and being swept into his arms.

The truth was sobering, for Molly had caught her reflection in the darkened window glass at night. Her features were strained and her clothing was limp and wrinkled. Not only that, ever since leaving Effingham, her thick hair had become increasingly unmanageable. Instead of looking as pristine as if she'd stepped from a bandbox, she bore a closer resemblance to something the cat had dragged in.

And although she was riddled with curiosity as to what her intended looked like, she was overwhelmed at the prospect of meeting a man who would mean so much to her. One who would fill her future so sweetly and completely.

She hoped.

So much depended upon his first impression of her! So after her arrival and before he ever laid eyes on her, she would have to rest, freshen up, and repair herself and her wardrobe from the rigors of the journey. Surely there was a hotel in Williams, she thought, not even daring to speculate on what course of action she would be forced to explore if no such establishment existed in the fledgling town!

When the freighter stopped at Cedar Spur, a few miles east of Williams, Molly saw only a town, a vast pole yard, and sheds. Her spirits plummeted. What if Williams were no bigger?

But it was!

"Oh, thank you, Lord," Molly murmured in a fervent whisper as the train chugged into town and ground to a halt, the passenger car squarely in front of the tiny depot building and the engine under the water tower beside the railbed.

Fired with renewed optimism, Molly hastily plucked up her luggage and prepared to disembark.

Williams was a small town, as Molly had expected, but only a block-and-a-half from the quaint burgundy and mustard-colored clapboard depot she spied a huge, three-story white-washed hotel, with a mercantile on the corner, a post office, a church, several residences, logging company offices, a black-smith shop, livery stable, a cobbler's shop, and several establishments that Molly couldn't identify from this distance. Near the edge of town was a black tar-paper shack, a tumble-down affair, but judging from the number of lumberjacks milling about, the establishment was doing a thriving business, aesthetics notwithstanding.

Only when she stepped down from the train did Molly suspect what *kind* of establishment it might be. For emanating from the yard was a series of curses, wails, bellows, and whacking thumps, signaling that a brawl was going on, and she knew, without having to be told, that the dilapidated building housed a . . . *saloon.*

Making her way carefully past the small knot of rough and

82

rugged men, Molly kept her eyes downcast. The raucous noise died away and silence hung heavy in the air. Without glancing up, she could feel the men's gazes, taking in every detail of her appearance.

"Bet that's her!" she overheard a lumberjack hiss, followed by the sound of expectoration as he spat a brown stream of tobacco juice on the ground nearby.

"Think so?"

"Yup. Has to be."

"Naw . . . that ain't her."

"What makes ya think it ain't?"

"Aw . . . I told ya she ain't comin', so like as not the trick's on you . . . snookered by a connivin' bit o' female pulchritude and a heartless businessman who'll steal away in the dead o' the night wit' your money, leaving nothin', not even a forwardin' address behind!"

Molly was relieved when her quick steps took her out of earshot before she could hear more. She'd hoped to slip quietly into town, all but unnoticed, and go about her business. But if they were discussing her, as she feared, then the marital transaction wasn't just a private matter between herself, her intended, and the brokerage firm in Chicago. And if the lumberjacks knew, then very probably the entire population was aware of the loveless matrimonial bargain she was about to strike.

Stepping gingerly so as to avoid the mud that seeped between the poles in the cordwood street, Molly proceeded directly toward the hotel. At close range, she could see a hand-painted sign hanging over the door—GRANT HOTEL—and stepped onto the porch.

She was wiping sweat from her forehead and trying to swat away a tenacious mosquito when a hefty woman appeared.

"How can I help you?" she inquired, smiling warmly and patting back a strand of hair that had escaped from the tight bun at the back of her head. "I'm Rose Grant and since I haven't seen you in these parts, I take it you're a newcomer to Williams."

"Yes, I need a room, please."

The woman eyed her quizzically. "For one night? Or do you plan to stay with us a spell? Rates are cheaper by the week."

"Then I'll pay for a week in advance," Molly said quickly. "After that . . ." Her words faded away. It probably wouldn't be wise to reveal the true nature of her business to a stranger.

She'd noticed after stepping down from the train and onto the weather-beaten railroad platform that she'd drawn the stares of curious onlookers who'd stopped suddenly in the midst of their conversation to stare at her and whisper in conjecture. New arrivals in the burgeoning village must not be an everyday occurrence.

"What brings you to Williams?" Mrs. Grant inquired pleasantly. "Got relatives at the lumber camp? A brother, perhaps, or maybe a husband you've come to join?"

"No . . . ," Molly replied hesitantly, "I'm a milliner by trade. I thought I might find work here."

"Oh! Well, we don't have a millinery shop yet, and I expect the womenfolk around here would be proud to have one. And I'll be among the first to patronize your place of business. My Sunday bonnet has seen better days, sad to say. The truth is, though, we've had to learn to do without many things we were used to back home, since they're hard to come by way out here."

"It was something like that where I came from in Illinois," Molly admitted, "although we're situated near a larger town ten miles away, and what we couldn't obtain there, we could order from Sears & Roebuck in Chicago."

"We're not that fortunate, I fear. What we need more'n anything are a dentist and a sawbones. We're lucky to have a few midwives and older women who're willin' to doctor folks and apply home remedies. And we womenfolk help one another when there's a birthin'. But I assure you, we'd treasure the arrival of a bonafide doctor. Last winter we lost a sweet young thing, the wife of one of the lumberjacks, when her firstborn came early."

A chill went through Molly when she considered her own mother's plight, how Sue Ellen Wheeler had died after giving birth to her twin daughters. Now that she was about to become a married woman herself, and probably a mother not long after, Molly wanted better for herself. "I'll be sure to add that to my petitions when I talk with the Lord," she said. "As the newest resident of this town, I, too, would rest easier if there was a man of medicine to tend to my needs and dispense apothecary preparations if the occasion arises."

"We'd all rest easier," Mrs. Grant murmured. "It doesn't take much of an injury in the woods to render it a fatal wound, if not from the injury itself, then from the infection that so often comes in its aftermath."

"Oh, I know," Molly agreed. "Down home, one of our neighbor gents very nearly succumbed to blood poisoning. But folks got him to a doctor in time and he pulled through, though a man of lesser constitution might be moldering in his grave."

"Life's harsh," the graying woman said, "and this untamed region makes survivin' a bit more chancy than it was back home." Mrs. Grant frowned as she consulted the register. "I'll tell you what, Miss Wheeler, I'll put you in the corner room on the third floor. It's got two windows, so you should be able to get a nice cross breeze to cool your room and make sleeping easier. The windows are screened, but even so, it seems those pesky mosquitoes manage to find a way in, so you'll find a mosquito netting to cover yourself so's you can sleep."

"I appreciate it," Molly replied sincerely. "I've never seen such huge mosquitoes."

"They're terrible this time o' year. The lumber company sometimes builds a smudge out of straw, but it covers the town with a pall of smoke. I don't know which is worse—the bites from the mosquitoes or the smoke stingin' your eyes to tears! Our poor baby is miserable even with the netting over her cradle." The stout woman caressed her abdomen. "I'm hoping that come next summer, when our next wee one comes, the pesky insects won't be so bad."

Molly's eyes grew round. "How wonderful," she murmured, "that you're in the motherly condition."

The tired-looking woman didn't seem so sure that the new addition was cause for elation. "I just hope I feel better then than I do now."

"You must get terribly tired."

"More tired than a body has a right to feel," Mrs. Grant sighed. "There's always so much to do in a day's time. And right now the young'uns are too small to be of much assistance.

"Well," she brusquely changed her tone and the topic, "I expect you've got better things to do than listen to my woes. Here's your room key, Miss Wheeler," she said, laying it on the marble countertop with a soft clunk. "I hope your stay with us will be enjoyable. You're welcome to remain here as long as you have a need."

Molly took the key. "Much obliged. I'll let you know my plans when I'm certain myself. Things are a bit up in the air right now." By nightfall of the following day, Molly was thinking, she would surely have discovered the course of her immediate future.

As she trudged up the stairs to her quarters, laden with her valise, satchel, and the canvas tote of rose starts, Molly determined that as late as it was, she was going to freshen up, see about getting something to eat, then spend the evening preparing herself for the next day when she appeared at the lumber company to meet her intended.

Until then, she dared think no further ahead.

chapter
7

Molly surveyed the neat corner room that was to be her home for the next week and a half and was surprised at what she saw. The room was exquisitely, if economically furnished, and she found herself impressed with Rose Grant's taste in appointments. She hadn't really expected such a delicate touch from the heavyset woman who, Molly felt, had rather "let herself go," appearing older than her actual age.

The airy room was blessed with natural light and gleaming hardwood floors, so shiny from waxing that Molly could see her reflection. The bed linens on the spindle bed were snowy white, crisply starched, and inviting to the touch, covered with a crocheted ivory bedspread over a plump, quilted eiderdown comforter.

Molly felt her spirits lift as she placed her worn leather Bible on the nightstand, then began to unpack her valise, hanging away her few garments and stowing her personal effects in drawers of the walnut marble-topped dresser that matched the bedstead.

On a walnut desk tucked off in a corner was a powder blue vase containing a bouquet of pink flowers arranged with a spray of lush, green fern. Molly had never seen the unusual blossoms before, and she made a mental note to ask Mrs. Grant about them.

Lovingly, proudly, Molly placed the fabric for her wedding gown and the matching trim, plus her few sewing accessories, into a roomy bottom drawer of the dresser. Come the morrow, she would begin to sew, once she had made a trip to the lumber company to meet her bridegroom, vowing that she would work day and night if necessary to finish it in time for her wedding day. Her eyes shining with hope, Molly stroked the beautiful, satiny material one last time before she slid the heavy drawer closed.

When she turned away, her countenance, reflected in the beveled mirror above the gleaming marble top, where she'd arranged her comb and hairbrush, radiated a vision of happiness. Somehow her eyes looked brighter, her cheeks rosier, her lips a deeper shade of pink. Tired as she was, Molly believed she'd actually never looked prettier.

From having read some of Marissa's Penny Dreadful novels, Molly knew that some claimed that starry eyes and rosy cheeks were a natural effect of being in love. But how could that be . . . when she had never even laid eyes on the man who was to be her husband?

Still, Molly could easily picture herself gowned in shimmering ivory and lace, a wispy, translucent veil obscuring her virginal features until, at the altar, her intended would lift the veil to gaze upon her with love. She could see it all now—a scene as breathtaking as the perfect, happy ending to a storybook.

But Molly's imagination always stopped there, for she could see herself as a beautiful bride, but she was never able to envision the man who would become her bridegroom.

Molly knew his name—Luke Masterson—but she had no idea if Luke was short or tall, lean or husky, handsome or plain, dark-complected or fair, boisterous or soft-spoken, highly intelligent or dull. And she knew his occupation—timber boss for Meloney Brothers Lumber Company. But she knew nothing else except that he wished to marry her. For her, it was enough. The fact that he wished to take her for his wife—to love, cherish, protect, and care for her—was all that mattered.

There was comfort in knowing that a man with a good job was in the market for a wife and was earnest enough about locating a life's partner that he had already tendered payment to a Chicago marriage broker. Here in this remote outpost, where marriageable women were in short supply, such an idea seemed practical.

Molly glanced at her timepiece for the fifth time in as many minutes. The hands on the ornate watch that had belonged to Sue Ellen Wheeler, seemed to drag by as Molly waited for the dinner hour to arrive at the hotel. She was tempted to slip downstairs and spend a bit of time with Rose Grant. Maybe she could even offer to help the overworked woman so as to allow some conversation. But fearing that Mrs. Grant would ask questions that would result in Molly's revealing more than she was prepared to tell, she chose to remain in her quarters.

When the supper hour finally came, Molly went downstairs, becoming woefully tongue-tied and flustered under the scrutiny of the other diners. And, after dinner, instead of seeking out companionship in the parlor off the main lobby, she scurried back to the privacy of her own room once again.

So tense was she about the outcome of the next morning's visit to the lumber company that Molly doubted she'd be able to sleep a wink. But to her surprise, after a long, luxuriating bath, she slipped into bed, read a chapter or two from her Bible, and dozed off, sleeping as one drugged.

She didn't awaken until a racket outside the hotel—lumber crews heading for the woods outside the sleepy town, she later learned—interrupted her rest. Molly rose hastily, attended to her hair and face, and dressed for the day.

At breakfast, prepared by Mrs. Grant, she found the poor woman looking wan and woozy—the effects of morning sickness caused by the coming babe, Molly suspected. Consulting her timepiece, her heart sped up when she realized that office hours for the lumber company a few blocks down the same street, would soon begin. And unable to bear the tension a moment longer, Molly exited the dining room and adjourned to her room to pace.

When at last Molly descended the staircase, she ran into Rose Grant leaving the kitchen. The woman looked flustered, but she put on an air of determined cheerfulness when she saw Molly. "You're just in time to have a cup of coffee . . . or even a little more breakfast, my dear. I noticed your appetite was off a bit earlier this morning. There are plenty of leftovers; tasty, too, if I do say so myself."

Molly smiled and shrugged. "You're a wonderful cook, Mrs. Grant. So there's no bragging in stating an honest fact. Your food is among the best I've ever eaten."

The woman seemed inordinately pleased, as if few compliments ever came her way. "Well, thank you, my dear. If there's anything I love, it's feeding folks with hearty appetites. So come in and join me!"

Since it was still not quite time to leave for the lumber company, Molly obediently trailed in her wake. "I really don't think I could swallow another bite, Mrs. Grant."

"Well then, come keep me company while I get off my feet and take my morning repast. And by the by, please call me Rose. It seems more friendly-like."

"If you'll do me the honor of calling me Molly."

"I'd be delighted, Molly," Rose Grant said, smiling warmly. "My, my, wasn't that a deal struck easy enough?"

"It certainly was," Molly agreed, joining the older woman in soft laughter as they made their way through the deserted kitchen still warm from the stove and rich with the swirling odors of food.

"There's plenty of vittles in the warmin' oven if you find out you can make room for another morsel. These days I wait and eat after I've fed folks in the morning, for while I'm cookin', I'm wonderin' if I'll ever desire a bite of food again, as poorly as I feel with this coming child. Thank the good Lord, my appetite returns later in the mornin'," she said, seating herself on a solid chair as Molly took a place across from her. "I'm eatin' for two these days, you know."

Judging from the woman's girth, Molly figured she must have been eating for two when there was no need. But she'd never venture such an observation to this good-hearted soul, even if she was shockingly obese.

"More coffee?" Rose was asking.

"I'll get it," Molly said, quickly arising. "You take your ease. Is there anything I can fetch for you while I'm up?" she asked, retrieving the speckled enamel coffeepot simmering on the huge wood range that seemed to take up all the space along one wall of the kitchen.

In addition to the large cooking surface, there were warming ovens and reservoirs to heat water, as well as ovens for baking all the food to feed the hotel's clientele and any customers who stopped in for a meal.

"A bit of heavy cream for my coffee, if you please," Rose replied gratefully. "It's in the icebox over beside the woodbox."

"Coming right up!" Molly called.

She poured herself coffee, served Rose Grant, then sat down again opposite the woman.

Because cream had been a rarity in the country, with butter considered more important, Molly had become accustomed to drinking her coffee black. She noticed that Rose poured the rich cream with a heavy hand until the color was almost as pale as the ivory material destined to become Molly's wedding gown. Then Rose dropped in several sugar cubes until the coffee level rose almost even with the lip of the cup. She waited an instant for the cubes to begin to melt, then took a little sip of the sweet, hot brew.

"Ah . . . I feel better already!" Rose breathed with satisfaction. "It's heaven to be able to take a moment for myself after feedin' all those lumberjacks and hotel patrons all mornin'."

"You work very, very hard," Molly observed.

"That I do. But it's necessary if there's to be any kind of life for us and our young'uns."

Molly had been wondering where Mr. Grant kept himself. "Do you have help at the hotel?"

Rose shrugged. "Oh, every now and again. But I'll have to have more before long, that's for certain." She gently patted her stomach that would soon swell with the growing baby's bulk. "But we tend to get by with what the family can provide. It's cheaper that way. And my Albert is known in these parts as a 'thrifty' man." Rose lowered her voice. "But between you and me, I think the man's as tight as bark on a tree. Why, 'tis a wonder he doesn't squeak when he walks!"

"Really?" Molly was amazed that Rose Grant would take her into her confidence on so short an acquaintance. At the same time, she was a little uncomfortable being privy to the subtle disharmony of a marriage that she would, otherwise, have deemed "a match made in heaven." Just like the unions at the end of each Penny Dreadful novel.

"Oh, he's a good man, don't get me wrong," Rose put in quickly. "But, like other men, he has his faults. But then," she added in an upbeat tone, "I have my shortcomings, too." As if to prove it, the heavy woman reached for another corn muffin, slathered it with butter, and drenched it in syrup. Tucking a stray wisp of hair behind her ear, she finished, "Mayhap that's why we make a good pair."

Molly nodded. "Perhaps." She didn't know what else to say, for the marital state was alien to her experience. The fact that she would soon know filled her with trepidation that gnawed away at the peace and happiness that had filled her only recently.

"What are your plans this mornin'?" Rose asked as she attacked the corn muffin and then forked a cold sausage patty from a platter nearby and topped it with a bit of horseradish before popping it into her mouth.

"I have to visit a few of the business places in Williams," Molly explained, feeling a bit guilty at this deliberate evasion when dear Mrs. Grant had been so forthright with her.

"Well, mention my name, iffen you think it'll do you any good," Rose invited.

Molly murmured her thanks. Perhaps she *would* mention Rose Grant to Luke Masterson. She knew he had partaken of meals at the hotel, and this would give them common ground on which to converse during those first difficult moments.

"It looks to be a gorgeous day," Rose said as she made short work of another muffin, which was now so cool that the butter failed to melt into the delicate, crumbly tenderness of its texture. The dash of syrup slid from the buttery surface and spilled to the plate, but the woman resolutely forked the muffin around, sopping up the sweet confection. "Sure you don't want a muffin?"

Molly, who felt a strange empty sensation in the pit of her stomach, needed no further prodding. Maybe a little something to eat *would* make her feel better. At least, it seemed to have improved Rose's overall constitution. "I don't mind if I do. But only one . . . for I must be going."

A muffin, delicious even cold, and another cup of steaming coffee did seem to magically revive Molly and improved her frame of mind so she felt more confident about the morning's encounter.

"Now I really should be setting about my business," she said at last, scraping her kitchen chair away from the work-table that had served as their dining table.

She was unaware of her heavy sigh punctuating the remark until Rose Grant remarked upon it. "I do declare, girl, you seem nervous as a cat this morning."

Molly suddenly felt nakedly revealed, although she was modestly dressed from head to toe. "Heavens!" she blurted. "It shows?!"

Rose gave a laugh that jiggled the folds of flesh under her chin. "A little," she admitted, reluctant to say more for fear of offending her guest or intensifying her anguish.

Strained silence fell between them.

"If something's troubling you, dear girl," Rose said softly, "you can unburden yourself to me if you think it'll help I told you more'n I generally say to others, 'specially the womenfolk in this town. But I sensed I could let down my hair with you without havin' to safeguard my speech."

"Oh, and you were right!" Molly insisted. "You need not fear that I'll divulge a word to anyone."

"Just know then, whatever your problems, you're not

alone." Rose gave Molly a level look. "I've had a long life—'most forty years—and it's taught me a heap about this tryin' world. More'n most folks, I sometimes think."

There was a sudden heavy sadness in the woman's eyes that Molly found chilling, for it was as if a curtain had suddenly risen, allowing her to look behind the cheerful façade. Now she knew that Rose Grant's stubborn optimism was only a careful presentation, an act. As if Rose were some character in one of the Shakespearean plays Miss Abby had read to them at school, playing her part flawlessly.

Molly sank back into the chair she had abandoned a moment before and gratefully accepted the steaming cup of coffee Rose had poured her. Wrapping her hands around the heavy mug, she warmed her hands, feeling a thawing of the chill that had pervaded her entire being. "I *am* nervous," she confessed.

Then, as if her tongue had taken on a life of its own, Molly rushed on, offering a litany of mitigating factors that had brought her to Williams, having made the decision to become a mail-order bride, intent on marrying a perfect stranger. The confession poured forth in a flood of emotion—much more than she'd ever intended to utter.

When she finished, Rose Grant, who never seemed at a loss for words, was speechless. But her kind eyes were shiny, filmed with unshed tears.

Molly was instantly contrite. "I–I'm sorry. I shouldn't have burdened you."

She was about to rise and leave the woman in peace, but Rose laid a restraining hand on her arm. "Oh, you've good reason to feel nervous, my dear. I well remember those self-same feelings. No one else in this town knows it, for I'm not proud of the fact . . . but I, too, Molly, was a mail-order bride."

Molly turned a disbelieving look on the woman. "You were?"

"Oh, yes, if the truth be known, I expect that fully half of us happily married womenfolk in this town had their origins the same as you and I. And *all* of the *un*happily married ones."

It was a sobering thought. If Rose Grant considered herself among the *happily* wed, Molly thought with alarm, what, oh what, must be the lot of those poor creatures who were visibly unhappy?

"There aren't many women to be found in these parts, Molly. Most of the menfolk who have a hankerin' for a woman to share their bed and board pursued the same mercenary route followed by your intended."

Molly nodded, but was unable to speak for the lump of fear in her throat and the unbidden tears that threatened to spill from her eyes.

"You haven't said yet, my dear, who the lucky man is who's to claim you for his bride."

"I . . . uh . . ." Molly stammered, feeling daft. "His name is Luke Masterson. He–he works for Meloney Brothers and . . ."

Rose erupted in a delighted little squeal. "Oh, I know Luke! Well, *that's* a relief! Until you mentioned his name, I feared you'd agreed to become the wife of one of the ne'er-do-well polecats that swell this town's population."

Molly brightened. "Then my intended . . . Luke . . . is a good man?"

"One of the best, I'd wager. It's for sure you'll never want for material things, my dear, unless Luke's as 'thrifty' as my husband, Bert. At least, you'll never do without because there's any lack of money."

"That's comforting to know," Molly admitted. But there were other traits that she valued even more. "Tell me, is he a church-going man?" she asked casually, as her heartbeat escalated within her breast.

Rose frowned, causing Molly's hopes to plummet. "Well," she said carefully, "I don't know as how I'd be a proper judge of that. Luke doesn't warm a pew as regularly as a body might like. But I do know he casts his shadow across the church doors at least once or twice a year . . . which is more than you can say for most of the men in this town, my Bert included."

"Has he an even temperament?" Molly ventured.

Rose shrugged and spread her hands. "He's as easygoing as a lot of men, and probably better-tempered than most. And he doesn't appear to be the kind of feller who'd lay a hand on a woman in anger, if that's what you mean."

Molly nodded, relieved, until Rose spoke further. "But then, who's to know for sure 'cepting a woman who'd lived intimately with him? Some of the men in this town aren't above disciplinin' a wife as they would an errant child."

Molly sighed. "Well, then, I guess I'll just have to hope for the best."

But Rose wasn't finished. "I do know that the men sometimes grumble about Luke. Rumor has it he's a firm taskmaster . . . some might even say harsh. But my view is he doesn't ask his men to do anything he isn't willin' to do himself. He's a fair man. And just. Reasonable, too. At least, he's always been courtly to me and the girl who used to come in durin' dinner hours to help out."

Molly was relieved. "He's a gentleman, then?"

"I'd say so. Of course, the same can be said of Bert, though I know the faults outsiders can't see, God love his soul!"

Molly felt as if she were on one of those roller-coaster contraptions she'd read about. For with one remark, Rose would lift her spirits to the skies, and in the very next breath, send her spiraling to a new low.

"As I'd size up the bloke," Rose went on, "I'd say he's salt of the earth. And in these parts, even a feller with some faults can still be a man among men by comparison. Luke's a good catch, Molly. You could do a lot worse, my girl. And he's certainly appealin' to the eyes. In fact . . ." Rose suddenly fell silent.

"Yes?" Molly prodded when the silence persisted.

The woman took several quick breaths, sighing in what seemed to be consternation, as if hesitating to speak further.

"In fact . . . what?" Molly coaxed.

Rose popped a cold piece of sausage into her mouth and chewed quickly, then washed it down with what remained of her heavily sweetened coffee. "Now please understand, Molly, that I don't mean to be unkind. But . . . well . . . Luke Masterson is a handsome man, so attractive, actually, that it's fairly surprisin' to me that he's arranged to acquire a bride through a marriage broker."

Molly didn't say anything. Couldn't.

Helplessly Rose stared at her, as if wishing Molly would speak up, if only to take the onus from her beefy shoulders. "Truth to tell, Molly, there's some of the saloon girls, and them right pretty bits of fluff, who'd think they'd done a good day's work if they could snare the interest of an eligible man like Luke Masterson. Not to be unkind, but he could have his pick of most of the women in this town. So, I'll admit, I'm findin' all this a bit of a puzzlement. Oh, I could understand it if he'd ordered hisself a dazzlin' beauty. But I am more than a little confused . . . well, *surprised* . . . that he's picked *you*."

At that moment, Molly was beyond feeling hurt. She knew Rose wasn't judging her physical attributes. Her new friend was just genuinely curious. "I–I'll have to admit I was thinking along the same lines myself."

Rose was immensely relieved that Molly hadn't taken offense and she hastened on. "Well, dear, very likely Luke Masterson is too smart to fall for just a pretty face or a beguilin' figure. Maybe he's got more to him than that. Maybe he's a feller who appreciates and cherishes the traits possessed by a good and godly woman."

"That's what I've been hoping . . . and praying."

"Don't trouble yourself overly much, dear," Rose said, realizing how quickly their conversation had progressed from a need for female companionship to intimate sharing of a painful concern. "I'm sure it'll all work out for good."

"I do hope so," Molly sighed and was surprised to hear Rose chuckling.

"Leastways, I have no fear that you'll meet the same dreadful fate as one bride who blew into these parts."

"Wh–what happened to her?" Molly asked, not sure she wanted to know.

"Well, when the gal—city born and bred—arrived on the inbound train, her feller was at the depot to meet her when she stepped from the dusty coach. But she took one look at him and blanched as white as the snow coverin' the ground. She let out a shrill 'Eeek!' like she'd just had a mouse run up her petticoats. Then she turned on her heel and ran back into that coach, bag and baggage, leavin' the smelly varmint standin' on the platform with his mouth wide open. Served him right, I'd say. For he was straight from the woods, with not the decency even to take a bath or groom his beard. The sight of him would've been enough to turn any woman's complexion pale as clabbered milk."

"My goodness!" Molly gasped.

"She was out of that lumberjack's life as fast as the engineer could throw the locomotive into gear again." Molly couldn't help grinning. "That lumberjack stood on the platform, as dumb as a poor beast who'd been struck 'twixt the eyes with a mallet. Reckon he couldn't believe his eyes. He stared after that train—and his woman—disappearin' into the distance and let fly a volley of curses like the good women of this town had never heard. Then he went to the saloon, where he commenced to drown his sorrows. And before the establishment closed for the night, he'd touched off a barroom brawl that cost him the lobe of his right ear . . . which didn't do a thing for his overall appearance, if I may be that uncharitable."

In spite of herself, Molly laughed out loud. "Then what happened?"

Rose shrugged. "Well, it would come as no surprise to learn that the next day the 'jacks didn't haul out the logs they're accustomed to handlin' in a day's time. The way that varmint was weepin' and wailin' over losin' the love of his life was a pure distraction. But from what I've heard, he got over it. Now, instead of spendin' money on a mail-order bride, he squanders it on liquor and loose women. And he's not alone."

Molly felt a wave of revulsion. "How awful."

"Mebbe so. But think how much worse 'twould have been for that delicate young girl to have stayed around and wed the old reprobate, and been expected to bear his children, to boot! No doubt, leavin' was the best decision she ever made."

"I–I guess you're right," said a sober Molly, growing more concerned by the moment.

"And if the truth be known, I expect there've been a few other mail-order brides who've considered gettin' back on the train, but didn't, if only because there was nowhere else to go and no money to take them there. And they've lived to regret it to this day."

Molly shuddered, thinking that this could well be her lot.

"Old as I am now, and having lived through all I have, I can't help but feel that a woman alone is better off findin' her own way in the world than marryin' a man she doesn't love and who isn't loved by him, either. In my estimation, true love's worth waitin' for."

When Rose finally ended her long monologue, Molly wasn't ready to tender a quick good-bye and set about her day's business, which now held even less appeal than before. In order to delay the moment, she spoke. "Have there ever been any women turned away by the men who've ordered them . . . when they got a good look?" Molly asked, voicing her worst fear.

"Heavens, no! Why, as rare as it is for a man to encounter available women in this wilderness, I expect a gal could be ugly as a gargoyle and still find herself a man to marry."

Molly felt sudden relief.

And sharp-eyed Rose Grant noticed. She reached across and patted Molly's plump arm that seemed downright skinny compared to Rose's own fleshy wrist. "You've no cause to fear, darlin'," she assured her. "You're a sweet-faced lass. Solid of body, yes, but obviously easy of temperament and willin' to work hard and tend a good home for a man to return to at eventide. Now don't you worry. Smooth your hair, bring a smile to that sweet face, and march on over to

Meloney Brothers Lumber Company and meet that man who's goin' to become your husband. There's no time like the present, Molly," Rose urged, boosting her bulk from the ladderback chair as she turned toward the sink and trailed her fingers through the water in the reservoir, testing its temperature.

Looking back over her shoulder toward Molly, who had made no move to leave, Rose gave a wave of her hand. "Be off with you! Think happy thoughts and don't drag yourself down, wonderin' why Luke Masterson wasn't at the depot to meet you. Now that you're here, he'll be right glad to see you!"

chapter
8

THE AIR WAS crisp and bracing when Molly closed the lobby doors of the Grant Hotel behind her and stepped out onto the street.

Pausing momentarily to collect her bearings and realizing she couldn't postpone the moment any longer, she sighed heavily and proceeded in the direction of the lumber company offices up the street. *Please, God,* she prayed, *please let Luke Masterson be happy to see me. And don't let me find disappointment in his eyes.*

Molly's heart seemed to thud louder with each step she took. She was hardly able to concentrate on her prayerful thoughts for the dizzying possibility of imminent failure. And by the time she was half a block away from the entrance to the clapboard lumber office, she was feeling short of breath and lightheaded.

At that moment Molly wanted nothing so badly as to turn around and flee in the opposite direction. But she'd come this far—one thousand miles—and she couldn't turn back now.

Gripping her hands together so tightly that the knuckles whitened, she gritted her teeth and stepped up to the door. Her lips quivered in wordless prayers for a miracle in the moments ahead.

And she considered it a miracle indeed when she found the strength to push open the door. A bell tinkled overhead and then jangled again when she solidly closed the door behind her, securing it against the brisk breeze, and she stepped near the tall, pot-bellied stove, ornate with chrome, that glowed with a coal fire winking orange from behind the isinglass panes in its opening.

She glanced around, hoping to find someone to direct her to Luke Masterson's office. Several men, obviously employees of the lumber company, eyed her with interest. They were dressed in uniform sameness—work-worn brogans, tan breeches, and plaid woolen shirts, with ragged knit hats pulled down over their foreheads. They seemed poised for action, apparently ready to get a late start on their day's labors in the big woods—handling teams of draft horses, bucking two-men crosscut saws, or working to repair broken implements in the smithy's shack.

Right now they were viewing Molly openly, elbowing each other surreptitiously, giving almost imperceptible nods as if intent on remaining long enough to eavesdrop on some conversation that would tell them what had brought her to this office ordinarily frequented only by men.

"May I help you, Miss?" asked the company clerk, a middle-aged, ruddy-faced man wearing a green eyeshade when he finally noticed her presence.

Molly cleared her throat. But when she spoke, she was unnerved to discover that her voice, even to her ears, sounded thin and reedy. "I–I'm here to see Mr. Luke Masterson," she said. "I've personal business to transact with him."

The clerk looked her up and down. "I see," he said hesitantly. "Uh . . . I'm sorry, Miss. He's . . ."

Molly's heart sank anew when she realized that the clerk was about to inform her that the timber boss was not in his office. "I co–could come back later," Molly ventured, hastily turning away.

106

"Wait, Miss," the ruddy-faced man called after her. "Mr. Masterson should return at any moment. Ordinarily he'd be here at this hour of the morning, but there's been a fracas at one of the lumber camps a few miles from town, and he was called away before dawn."

"I see . . . ," said Molly, concluding that her husband-to-be was as important a man as the marriage broker had led her to believe.

"Is there anything I can do to help?" the clerk inquired in a solicitous tone. "I'm authorized to act for Mr. Masterson in certain matters."

Molly flushed helplessly, as if the clerk were somehow privy to her thoughts. "No. Sorry. B–but thank you kindly," she demurred in a pleasant tone, managing to give him a quick smile. "I'm here to discuss a very private matter with Mr. Masterson. It's not company business, nor is it terribly pressing. Another time will be just fine. Perhaps tomorrow. Or even the day after. I'm sure he's a very busy gentleman."

"That he is. I could make an appointment," he offered, consulting a register. "Or leave a note on his desk for Mr. Masterson to contact you."

"Oh, that won't be necessary," Molly said hastily, only wanting to conclude the whole embarrassing ordeal.

"Right you are, ma'am," the clerk cheerfully agreed, "for you're in luck. I just heard the clip-clop of Mr. Masterson's saddle horse. As soon as he tethers his mount to the hitching post out back, he'll be in. I'm sure he'll have a few minutes to spare to attend to your business. Please wait here."

No sooner had he spoken than a door to the rear of the drafty building opened with a bang, then thudded shut, rattling on its hinges.

Realizing that the time of their meeting was at hand, Molly

felt a swoony faintness sweep over her and she clutched the countertop for support as she prepared herself for her first glimpse of the important, and if Rose Grant was to be believed, the incredibly handsome man who was soon to become her legally wedded husband. And, she hoped fervently, her dearly beloved mate.

But Molly was further disappointed, for moments passed and Luke Masterson failed to put in an appearance. Perhaps he had disappeared elsewhere within the building.

"Wait here," the clerk instructed, "and I'll fetch Mr. Masterson to the counter." He pivoted away, intent on fulfilling his promise.

"No . . . please!" Molly cried out and was stricken by the almost shrill desperation of her tone. She swallowed hard, striving to modulate her speech. "Is . . . there a more private area where we—Mr. Masterson and I—could converse? It's . . . very important." Molly felt her cheeks flame until she knew they had turned the color of brick.

The clerk shrugged. "His office, then," the man replied. "Come with me and I'll tell him you're here."

The man paused midstep, gesturing for Molly to come around the end of the scarred counter and follow him down a short, dim hallway. He hesitated outside a closed door, and Molly hung back, seeking shelter in the shadows.

Adjusting his eyeshade, the portly man rapped on the door. "Sir? A young woman's here to see you."

"What does she want?" came the tired, faintly exasperated response.

"I don't know, Mr. Masterson. She claims it's a personal matter, and she'd like to see you privately."

There was a sigh of resignation that was sufficiently heavy to carry through the closed door. "Very well. Show her in."

Molly's heart sank. She could hear not only resignation but exhaustion in Luke Masterson's voice and sensed that he'd had little sleep the night before, and that whatever the fracas that had called him to the lumber camp before dawn, it had been a frustration to him.

Molly feared that these were not the best circumstances under which to introduce herself to her intended, but that couldn't be helped. Why, she thought, and her spirits lifted a little, perhaps her arrival would actually play a part in putting Luke Masterson in a better frame of mind. Perhaps the postponements she'd suffered along the way had filled him with as much anxiety as she, and he was equally as eager to meet her as she was to meet him.

"Go right in, Miss," the clerk said, twisting the doorknob, then quickly stepping aside to allow Molly Wheeler entrance into his employer's inner sanctum. Then, after giving Molly an uncertain smile, the man quickly departed for the front of the building.

Left on her own, Molly struggled for the composure to present a brave face to the gentleman whose back was turned to her. She so wanted to make a good first impression.

"Come in and have a chair," Luke said, swiveling back to his desk but continuing to peruse the paperwork in his hand, not even glancing at her as he gestured blindly in the general direction of an oak chair. The dull green cushion was soiled, as if it had borne the weight of many a hefty lumberjack. A brass spittoon, strategically placed, was mute testimony to the fact that women seldom visited this office.

"Now what can I do for you?" he said at last, looking up.

When their eyes met, Molly felt as if all speech had fled. She stared helplessly, her mouth working. But no sound came out.

Luke Masterson was every bit as appealing as Rose Grant had claimed. Maybe more so! He was tall—as tall as Pa, and her late father had been a giant of a man. His shoulders were as broad as Alton Wheeler's, too, and he had the same dark hair, although it was cut differently. Though Luke Masterson obviously spent many hours working in the company offices, his well-toned body gave evidence that he could also perform hard labor in the woods, side by side with the toughest loggers in the business.

His eyes were a deep blue and rimmed with thick, long lashes that almost seemed a waste on a man. His chin was dented with an appealing cleft, and his lips were finely chiseled, though Molly could only wonder at what a smile would do for his features, since his dark brows remained furrowed in a frown. A handlebar mustache, neatly waxed, turned up at the corners.

Unbidden, the thought occurred to Molly that she and Luke Masterson were the perfect pair to represent a natural phenomenon in the bird world—the fact that God created the hen to be plain so that she could hide securely on her nest, while the male of the species strutted proudly in all his fine plumage, the better to draw attention from his mate.

Molly had no notion how long she'd been staring until Luke Masterson's question jolted her from her musings. "You have business with me?" His tone was curt, urging her to get to the point and then kindly remove herself from his office so he could get about his work.

She finally found her voice. "I'm Molly Wheeler, Mr. Masterson."

"Wheeler . . . Wheeler," he mused softly, almost under his breath, as if he were trying to jog a mental note and come up with a clue as to her identity and the nature of her business with him. He even glanced at the four-drawer file cabinet, snugged in one corner of the office, as if he might be considering opening it in hopes of extracting a file under her name.

"I only arrived in Williams yesterday," Molly supplied helpfully, hoping to ease the tense moment that was even worse than she'd feared in her most awful imaginings. "I came from Effingham, Illinois."

"That was certainly a long trip," he sympathized. "And you're in Williams to see me? I'm sorry, but I'm afraid I don't understand."

Sensing that he was about to tell her that Meloney Brothers Lumber Company employed only men, Molly spoke up. "I'm *Molly Wheeler*," she repeated with pointed emphasis.

Mr. Masterson caught the inflection in her tone and his eyes flicked up from the paperwork in his hand. He circled his desk, perched on the edge, then thoughtfully regarded her, a quizzical expression on his handsome face. "Am I supposed to know you?"

Molly squirmed in misery. "Yes . . . no . . . well, I mean yes *and* no."

Masterson sighed with impatience. "Woman, would you please state your business in as clear and concise a manner as possible? I'm a very busy man and I don't have time for guessing games. These are my office hours, and this unscheduled call is not only inconvenient, but I'm beginning to suspect it is entirely social in nature. So I'm not sure this is the time and place for . . ."

Fighting the urge to flee, Molly sat there, knowing that her rubbery limbs would never carry her as far as the door. She was further horrified when she found herself talking rapidly—gibbering, actually—as she tried to explain. "I–I'm Molly Wheeler, you see, and I arrived in Williams late yesterday

afternoon to fulfill the terms of our marriage contract, nego-
tiated by Mr. Solomon Stein of Chicago, who is employed as
a marriage broker," she finished in a breathy whisper.

Luke's ruddy complexion drained pale. "What?!" he
gasped, his riveting eyes, orbs of blue-tipped steel that bore
right through her.

"I'm your mail-order bride, Mr. Masterson," Molly
announced weakly, her face suffused with hurt, humiliation,
and desperate courage.

A painful silence spiraled between them as Luke said nothing more and Molly was incapable of further speech.

"This is preposterous!" he said at last. "Are you daft? Have
you just escaped from some lunatic asylum? Surely you can't
be serious, my good woman!"

Molly wilted beneath his scathing look. The boneless sensation escalated until she was fearful that she might topple
from the chair, completely humiliating herself in front of the
shocked timber boss.

His disbelief seemed genuine. But then the awful thought
dawned that perhaps it was only a careful façade, and that he
was purposely pretending ignorance of the arrangement
rather than wound her further by rejecting her and sending
her packing.

Tears stung the back of Molly's eyes as she was unable to
wrest her gaze from Luke's unflinching stare. "I am . . ." she
gulped, swallowing hard. "I mean I *was* serious, Mr.
Masterson. I traveled to these parts in good faith and with
honorable intentions. But if you do not wish to go through
with our agreement, you'll get no argument from me."

His voice grew faint and reflective. "You really do sincerely
believe that I ordered you, don't you?"

Molly wiped away the quick tears that had pooled in her

eyes until the force of gravity caused them to spill over and trail a hot path down her flushed cheeks. "I'm rather helpless not to," she admitted, her tone flaring with unavoidable testiness, "since I completed the necessary paperwork the same as you."

Luke shook his head, his eyes still riveted on her. "I filled out no paperwork."

It was too much for Molly! "I have your letter right here!" she said, fumbling with the closure on her carpetbag. She glared defensively as she fished through her possessions and retrieved the bent envelope containing the missive she'd read and reread time and again until the paper was soft and feathery from so much handling. Producing it triumphantly, she handed it over with trembling fingers.

Mr. Masterson took it from her, withdrawing the letter, then flicking the single sheet open with a snap of his wrist that was lightly furred with dark, wiry hair. He gave it a cursory glance, then tossed it onto his desk. "I didn't write this," he said in a tone that was almost lethal in its quietness.

He arose, his abrupt motion sending his captain's chair rolling backward. And in a few quick strides, he crossed the room. A filing cabinet drawer clattered open and he withdrew a hefty, leatherbound book that looked like a ledger. This he slammed down on the side of his desk nearest her.

Fingering the gilt-edged pages, he plucked the book open to a random page and spread it wide for her examination. "Observe," he instructed, nodding toward the letter and then back at the ledger page. "You can see for yourself that the letter you claim I wrote was not penned in my handwriting. If you need further proof, my clerk can attest to the veracity of my statement."

"Oh, dear," Molly murmured when confronted with the evidence.

The neat script in the ledger, not the crude scrawl of the document she held in her hand, looked like that of a cultured and educated man like Luke Masterson.

"My guess," he said, "is that this distasteful epistle is the collaborative effort of a group of troublemakers, lumberjacks who were unable to accept the fact that I don't waste my time on wine and women as they tend to do."

"Oh, dear," Molly repeated in a wretched tone, feeling as if she were strangling.

"Miss Wheeler, obviously you've been snookered. You've become the butt of a cruel and malicious joke that's been perpetrated on you for some reason."

Molly gave a quick nod, for she didn't dare attempt speech. And what was there to say anyway?

Luke Masterson's frown deepened. "I think I even have a good idea just exactly who the culprits are, and when I find out, they'll pay for this. No doubt the rascals behind these shennanigans pooled what funds they hadn't squandered on loose women and cheap whiskey at the Black Diamond, and sent payment to the brokerage firm you mentioned. But I've never heard of the gentleman you claim arranged this unfortunate imbroglio. And I'd not need his assistance, no matter what the situation, for I'm not the marrying kind!"

"Oh, dear!" was all Molly could manage.

"I suspect the scoundrels ordered a bride for me in the mistaken notion that she—*you*—would improve my disposition." He gave a mirthless smile that did not reach his eyes. "It seems to be a widely held belief at some of the lumber camps, Miss Wheeler, that a wife is what I need to remove what some of the lumberjacks view as my rough edges and to make me more mellow and agreeable. But they're wrong! I have no need for you or any other woman on God's green earth. So don't waste your time, Miss Wheeler. I'm not the man for you, nor are you the woman for me. But take no offense, for no such woman has ever been created!"

Molly felt as if she'd been trapped in a horrendous nightmare from which it was impossible to awaken. In mere minutes her whole world had splintered apart, her dreams lying in shards around her, ground beneath Luke Masterson's polished boots. "Whatever will I do?" she asked softly, more of herself than of the man sitting across from her.

He shrugged. "I don't care *what* you do," he said, his tone little more than a whiplash. "Go or stay. Your course of action is of no concern to me. I had nothing to do with your arrival in this town, nor will I take any responsibility for how you leave. If you stay in this area—and I can't imagine for a moment why you would choose to do so—you'll be on your own. But it's only fair to warn you—this region offers rich opportunities to able-bodied men, but practically nothing for a woman, especially a woman alone."

Luke gave Molly an assessing look. "You're not . . . uh . . . cut out to be a saloon girl, it appears, although most of the men aren't particularly choosy, so you might get on there. Failing that, however, you might inquire about work as a scullery maid, for the proprietor of that establishment does serve meals to the 'jacks who are too inebriated to dine at the Grant Hotel."

Molly flinched. Then she felt a wave of fury sweep over her at the implication. "I'd die before I'd perform *that* kind of labor!"

Luke gave a nonchalant shrug. "Pardon me, Miss Wheeler, but the difference you claim is lost on me. You quail at the idea of selling your affections to many men . . . but you don't bat an eyelash about selling yourself to *one* man who is as unknown to you as the clientele who'd walk through the doors of the Black Diamond on any given day."

Molly glared at Luke through a film of tears that blurred her vision. "I did not come here to be insulted," she said, quickly rising to her feet.

Again Luke shrugged. "By your own admission, Miss Wheeler, you arrived on the scene, expecting to be married. Well, if you're so inclined, no doubt it can be arranged with some dispatch. This town's population is full of men longing for a woman—any woman—even a plain and buxom wench like yourself. If marriage is what you have in mind, girl, you can certainly hold out for it and find yourself properly hitched before the sun sets this very evening.'"

In response, Molly only wept all the harder.

"Make no mistake," Luke warned. "While I feel no personal responsibility toward you, I'm aware that it was my men—who will very likely find themselves no longer in my employ when I get to the bottom of this—who hoodwinked you into this predicament. So, if you wish, I can post a flyer announcing your intentions and the details regarding where you may be reached by interested parties."

Molly was livid. "Don't do me any so-called favors," she said acidly, finally able to choke out the words, as her hurt and anger seemed magically to dry her eyes. "Until the day I die, I shall consider myself blessed that you did not order me from the broker in Chicago! I'd rather remain a spinster all of my days than to spend them with you! For I need no man in my life to feel whole and fulfilled."

Luke gave her a tight smile. "That may be the most intelligent remark I've ever heard any woman make. As a breed, womanhood seems to specialize in silliness and lack of logic. You may just possess more innate intelligence than your sisters. You, Molly Wheeler, may be rather like I know myself to be—simply not the marrying kind!"

"Perhaps," Molly agreed stiffly, "for I realize now that I certainly wouldn't marry the likes of you . . . not even if you were the very last man on earth!"

Luke gave an amused chuckle and waved away her protest. "Have no fear of that, Miss Wheeler. Even if I *were* the last man on earth . . . I'd bite off my own tongue before I'd ever ask for your hand in marriage!"

Molly drew herself up to her full height, determined to give as good as she got and somehow find a way to leave this humiliating encounter with as much dignity as she could muster. "Well," she said softly, "as incompatible as we have discovered ourselves to be, at least we're in complete agreement on one count. Please forget my name as if you'd never heard it, and forget my face as if you'd never seen my features, and I give you my word that I shall do the same. Good day!"

With that, Molly turned on her heel and left Luke Masterson's office, painfully aware of her clumsy limp. She stared straight ahead, unseeing. But despite her vow, she could not erase the handsome, aloof, unattainable features that were branded on her mind.

Once safely outside on the street, there was no stemming the flood of tears provoked by a maelstrom of emotions—grief . . . fear . . . shame . . . fury . . . hurt. And Molly wept all the way back to the Grant Hotel and into Rose's solid, comforting arms.

chapter
9

"MOLLY, DARLIN', WHATEVER on earth is wrong? What happened that you're takin' on so?" Rose Grant folded her arms around the sobbing young woman and crushed her to her ample bosom.

Molly shook her head, unable to speak, and trembled with the wracking force of her tears. Her lower lip quivered and she hiccoughed as she tried to inhale a quick breath before she could frame a reply. "He–he doesn't want me!"

Rose looked thunderstruck. "No!" she cried in disbelief.

"Yes! And he never did want me, Rose! Oh, it's awful! I ca–came all the way from Illinois to Minnesota, bringing my dreams as well as my few belongings. And instead of finding the fulfillment of all my hopes, my arrival's proven to be the culmination of a cr–cruel joke, played by a gaggle of lumberjacks on their boss!" she ended on a wail.

Rose looked as if she'd been pole-axed. "A *joke?*"

Molly impatiently swiped at her tears. "Yes . . . a dastardly joke . . . b–but I don't think it's funny at all!"

"Doubtless neither does Mr. Masterson," Rose said in a soft, sympathetic whisper. "Oh, my poor girl. This is dreadful."

"I wish I could just die, I'm so mortified," Molly whimpered, straining not to give in to further tears.

"Come into the kitchen," Rose ordered in a pragmatic tone. "I know just what will make you feel better—a piece of cake, a handful of cookies, or a slab of pie just warm from the oven."

"Oh, I couldn't eat a bite," Molly protested. "My stomach is in knots."

Rose patted her on the shoulder. "Then food is exactly what you need. And I've made a fresh pot of coffee. It will help chase away that chill you're suffering in the face of such a shock. Come along now."

Molly followed Rose into the kitchen, feeling at home immediately. The warmth of the galley area was tantalizing with rich odors that emanated from the various pots and kettles bubbling merrily on the massive wood range, their lids lifting rhythmically before clinking down again with each puff of escaping steam.

On a sideboard nearby, several pies, a large apple cobbler, a wire basket of cooling cookies, and a freshly frosted triple-layer cake represented the bulk of Rose Grant's morning handiwork, assisted by her eldest daughter, thirteen-year-old Becky.

Rose gently pushed Molly down into the chair she'd vacated earlier. "What's your pleasure, my dear?" she asked, gesturing toward the brimming sideboard. "It's on the house."

"Nothing . . . really . . ." Molly said, but rose to pour herself a cup of coffee to prevent the pregnant woman from waiting on her hand and foot.

"Bosh!" Rose snorted. Ignoring Molly's protest, she filled a dainty china plate with several crinkly brown gingersnaps, glittering with granulated sugar, and set it before the girl.

Molly didn't plan to touch the delectable morsels but cupped the mug of coffee, drawing heat from it to ease the chill of rejection that seemed to penetrate to the very bone. But as she prepared to unburden her heart to her sympathetic friend, completely unaware of what she was doing, she picked up first one cookie, then another. And as she talked on about the disastrous episode with Luke Masterson at the lumber company, every cookie disappeared, until Rose got up to replenish the plate with another round for them both.

The combination of strong coffee and sugary cookies, not to mention Rose's sincere concern, did wonders for Molly's spirits. She was still sure she'd rather face death than lay eyes on Luke Masterson again. But somehow, fortified by the food in her system, the pain that had been like a knife plunging into her heart eased, almost as if she'd been given a bracing dose of laudanum.

"It was so humiliating," Molly whispered. "But what is ironic, Rose, is that as sorry as I felt for myself, I also pitied Mr. Masterson, who was every bit as much a victim of circumstances as I. And he with his day off to a woeful start already! Though I must admit, he had no empathy for what I was having to endure as a result of this cruel hoax."

"Males and females don't see things alike, honey," Rose explained, shrugging. "One thing I've learned about the opposite gender, from being married nigh on sixteen years, is that men view the world through a lens of hard logic. And women don't. We see with our hearts."

"I suppose so," Molly said with a sigh. "Luke just didn't seem to understand at all. He certainly *looked* the part of the gentleman you described to me, Rose. But he wasn't very nice. In fact, some of the things he said were downright beastly."

Her face scarlet, Molly shared Luke Masterson's unsympathetic suggestions about what she could do to provide for herself if she chose to remain in Williams. "I can't afford to move on," she said, "so I have no choice but to stay. Right now, I don't know what I'm going to do. But I'd die before I'd cast my lot with that of the fancy women who ply their trade at the Black Diamond Saloon!" She withdrew a linen handkerchief from her cuff and dabbed at her nose and eyes. "And, anyway, Mr. Masterson's right. I'm not pleasing enough to the eyes to be hired anyway."

Rose looked appalled. "It'd be over my dead body that I'd stand idly by and allow a fine Christian woman like yourself to be brought to such a state! Not while there's breath in my body!" Rose insisted. "What you're going to do, Molly Wheeler, is something I know you can do . . . and do well."

Molly's eyes flicked up in interest. The only vocation she really knew was the millinery trade, and it hadn't taken her long to realize that she'd never be able to support herself making fashionable bonnets for the area's few womenfolk.

"You can help me run the hotel!" Rose announced.

But Molly was adamant. "I cannot accept charity," she quietly demurred, "nor favors at your expense."

"Charity? Favors?" Rose stared at Molly in stark amazement. "'Twould not be *me* doing *you* a favor, girl. 'Twould be the other way around! Please, consider it! I'm not young any longer, Molly-girl. I've borne seven children and am in the family way with number eight. There's already days I can hardly drag my bones from bed to face my workday. But someone's got to provide for the family, and my husband, Bert, he isn't the most reliable of men. So that responsibility falls to my shoulders."

"You do work hard, Rose, much too hard," Molly admitted, "and you really should be taking your ease."

"Right you are!" said Rose. "But a business concern like ours allows a body precious little time for that! You start out runnin' a business, thinkin' you've got the world on a string.

But the day comes when you wake up and find you don't own the business so much as *it owns you!*"

"I'm sure that's true," Molly said, her tone reflective.

"The deed to this property may be in my husband's name," Rose said and her eyes sparked, "but anyone with the brains God gave a goose knows that *I'm* the one who keeps it goin', that it's *my* life's blood invested in this establishment. I need help, Molly Wheeler, and I'm going to have it. And you, my dear, are going to be our new full-time employee. Unless," Rose said quietly, "you decide to break my heart by turnin' me down. And I don't think you will. . . . After all, we're so much alike."

"We really are, aren't we?" Molly mused.

Rose gave a hearty sigh. "More than you realize, my dear, and someday when we've the time—and the privacy—I'll tell you my rather sad story. Mayhap then you'll thank the good Lord that Luke Masterson turned you down. But that can wait for another time. Right now, there's work to be done!"

"Of course," Molly said compliantly, rising to clear the dishes from the work table and carry them to the sink area. "What would you like for me to do first?"

"Come now," Rose teased. "I shan't have to instruct a smart gal like you. I can tell that a kitchen is your natural domain, same as it's mine. Just look around and see what needs doin', then turn your hand to it."

"Well . . . as a matter of fact," Molly began, grinning for the first time all day, "there are a few things I believe I can handle. If nothing else, it will free you up for other matters."

"Here's an apron." Smiling widely, Rose provided the garment before Molly could get the words out of her mouth.

"You know, Rose, I think this is really going to work," Molly said, tying the apron securely in place.

Rose folded the younger, smaller woman to her and gave her a bone-crushing hug. "I know it will! The good Lord doesn't make mistakes," she reminded Molly, "and it may just be that he sent you to Williams, not because Luke Masterson needed you, but because *I* needed you so desperately."

"No more than I need someone to be like a mama to me." Molly dared to speak her thoughts aloud, remembering Sue Ellen whom she'd never known, and even Miss Abby, who in her simple-minded confusion, had become more child than mother to her stepdaughters.

"I feel better already," Rose admitted as Molly set right to work, flawlessly and meticulously performing chores that until moments before had fallen to her. "It's true what they say about many hands making light work."

Molly turned a radiant smile on the grateful woman. "I have the most wonderful feeling that I'm going to be happy here, Rose."

"Lord willing. And it's guaranteed, if I have anything to do with it," Rose promised. "By the way, Molly, you accept your orders from me. I'm in charge in this hotel. If Bert happens to give you any trouble, just pay that meddlin', tight-fisted rascal no neverminds, all right?"

"Very well," Molly murmured, and tried to dismiss the prickle of alarm that suddenly penetrated the warmth that had enveloped her.

"You'll get your room and board free," Rose went on to explain. "And don't go sparin' the foodstuffs when you portion up your plate. We have a good business, and it's because I'm not stingy with the vittles. Same goes for my kitchen help. If it's there, eat up. I don't want to have to worry 'bout leftovers."

"I can help in other ways besides the kitchen duties, too," Molly volunteered. "Keeping up a hotel must be exhausting."

"I'll appreciate the help, darlin'. And the wages I pay you will show that, Molly."

"Wages, too!" Molly whispered, amazed at her good fortune.

"Of course!" Rose's tone was emphatic, making it clear that she'd brook no arguments in the matter. "A woman should have her own resources upon which to rely, so's she's not at the mercy of men . . . 'specially the godless blokes who treat a woman like a cheap trinket 'stead of a pearl beyond price."

"I'm so grateful to you, Rose. . . ." More tears threatened to spill, testimony to Molly's gratitude.

"You'll be worth the investment, my dear," Rose assured her. "And I'll find it satisfying to do for you like a mama. There'll be pleasure in knowin' that, in my own small way, I'm helping the Lord give you a little better life than these old bones of *mine* have ever known."

Molly was surprised. "But you seem so happy all the time," she protested, thinking of the ever-present smile on the woman's kind face.

"Many a woman has used a smile to shield her heartbreak from the world," Rose said sagely. "Bert gives me trials and tribulations to endure, but the Lord gives me my joy in life, 'long with the young'uns he's blessed us with."

Molly gave her a searching look, then decided to change the subject. "I'm so glad there's a church in Williams. Do you know the pastor and his family well?"

"Currently there is no pastor," Rose admitted. "We had one for awhile—and a grand and godly man he was, too—but family sickness called him away. It's been a sore loss. Some of the menfolk offer testimony, and we maintain our weekly services, but it's not the same as havin' a real pastor to minister to the flock."

"How disappointing it must be."

"We're hopin' for a replacement. Luke Masterson isn't much of a churchgoer. But one thing I can say about that man is that if this little town has a need, then Luke sets about to find a way to fill it. Rumor has it that he grew up in an orphan home with a fellow who went to seminary and went on to become a fine minister of the gospel. Luke's been in contact with his old boyhood friend, encouragin' him to bring his wife and children and come to Williams."

"Do tell!" Molly said. "Isn't it unusual for an unchurched man to make such an effort?"

"Not when you get to know Luke. He believes in the future of this town. And I know for a fact that he's tryin' to entice a bonafide physician to come to these parts, too. For he told me himself—one evenin' when he dined here—that he's hoping a new doctor will soon arrive in town and set up practice in time for my coming babe's birth." She sighed and Molly could see the exhaustion and fear Rose could no longer hide behind her careful smile.

"I had a right hard time with my last young'un. Sometimes I worry about dyin', Molly-girl, and leavin' my children with only Bert to rely on, and him not much of a father. The Lord knows my babes need me, so I'm hopin' he'll spare me 'til I can see my children raised up. Even if I don't live to dandle a grandbaby on my knee."

"You have me now," Molly said briskly. "And, Rose, you *are* going to take your rest. You need it . . . and the little one needs it. I ran the household for a timber boss in Illinois," Molly admitted, "and I did a good job of it, if I do say so myself. So this is work I'm accustomed to. With a hotel, there's only a little more of it. But the labor will do me good." Molly looked down at her own plump figure. "Besides, if I work a bit harder . . . and find a way to resist your wonderful fare so I eat a bit less . . . then perhaps I won't always be so . . . buxom . . . and might even become appealingly svelte."

"You'd never know it to look at me, girl," Rose said, lowering her gaze to take in her great girth, "but once upon a time, I was a little slip of a thing with an hourglass shape fit to turn the heads of many a gentleman on the street, modestly dressed though I was. Then I got married, began havin' my babes, and, as you can see."

"That does happen," Molly conceded.

"It's not just because I'm a prize-winnin' cook," Rose said thoughtfully. "I guess the real reason is because . . . 'cept for my young'uns and my faith in the Lord, food is the only pleasure I have in life . . . though I do have my memories." There was a wistful look on the woman's face. "I'll tell you about it sometime, like I promised."

Molly nodded, not daring to break into Rose's reminiscence.

"Don't let myself think of those times, 'cept once in a blue moon. Guess the reason is that the memories are so pleasurable it's too painful to leave 'em behind and face my realities."

"I see," Molly murmured, not seeing at all. What dreams had Rose Grant been forced to relinquish? What difficult choices had been thrust upon her?

Molly could only wonder and wait for the day when Rose Grant was ready to take her into her confidence.

"If only . . . ," Rose murmured as she set about peeling a huge mound of potatoes. "If only . . ."

chapter
10

"OUT WITH IT, Marissa!" Marc insisted, his gentle voice firm, his eyes dead serious. "You haven't been yourself in days. What's your problem?"

At his query, Marissa felt her anxiety and frustration beginning to mount again. She gave a shrug and looked around her helplessly, attempting to divert his attention elsewhere, away from the unpleasant truth she had intended to keep from Marc. "There's no problem . . . really!" she assured him with what she hoped was a convincing smile.

His response was a stern frown. "Now don't you become mulish and evasive with me, young lady! Your ruse might fool someone else, but I'm a physician, remember, trained to spot symptoms—both obvious to the eye and covert. And I say there's trouble!"

In answer, and hoping to purchase a moment in which to organize her chaotic thoughts, Marissa cleared her throat. "Please, Marc . . . I mean, Dr. Wellingham . . . what's troubling me really doesn't concern you."

Marc gave the young woman a look of incredulity. "Don't talk in circles, Marissa. And be assured that whatever concerns you most certainly *does* involve me. You're like a part of me, my dear. I can't imagine my life without you in it. I love you. I care about you. I feel responsible toward you. I want you to lean on me . . . just as I would hope that if I were in need, you'd be there for me to turn to. Now, out with it! What's bothering you?"

Marissa could not contain a deep sigh. "It's your mother."

"Mother?"

"Yes. Your mother," Marissa admitted miserably, "and Isabella, too, for she's had a hand in it."

Marc seemed confused. "But I thought the three of you were getting along famously."

Marissa shrugged. "After a fashion. Or, rather, I was honestly hoping we'd get along. But that doesn't seem to be the case."

Marc glanced around him, then gave a sweeping gesture to encompass the lavishly appointed room—the oriental rugs, the ancient brass artifacts, the latest and most costly in lighting inventions. Even the plumbing was a wonder to a girl accustomed to an outdoor privy, he knew. "Are you not happy here?"

Marissa had so treasured living in the lap of luxury that she viewed it as an honor, rather than her paid duty, to maintain the Wellingham abode, where she secretly pretended to be the lady of the manor.

"Thanks to you, the place looks better than it ever has before," he went on without waiting for her answer.

"I try," Marissa admitted, her countenance somber.

"And you succeed!" Marc insisted, detecting her bleak mood. "Mark my words, Marissa Wheeler, you're the best domestic help Mother's ever retained. So much so, my dear, that she considers you far more than a run-of-the-mill and easily replaced servant. I know my mother, my dear, and she's actually very much taken with you."

"I'm not so sure."

"Well, I'm positive of that diagnosis," he went on. "Mother has her moments, Marissa darling, I'll grant you that. She's afflicted with a middle-aged woman's . . . uh . . . ailments. And in addition, Father spoiled her outrageously. She was so pampered when he was living that she's completely self-centered. She's never known what it's like to do an honest day's labor . . . or what it's like to do without all the fripperies she considers important. But believe me when I assure you that she's treated you with far more favor than she usually bestows on hired help."

Marissa nodded. "She has been kind enough, as has Isabella. At least to my face. But . . ."

"Trust me, Marissa. Mother considers you a veritable gem. She's absolutely wild about you."

Marissa managed a smile and laid her hand lightly on Marc's forearm. "It's sweet of you to say so," she murmured, automatically straightening a cut glass objet d'art as she turned away. "And, to your credit, I realize that you actually believe that. But we women sense things."

"What are you driving at, my dear?" Marc murmured, frowning in speculation.

Marissa found herself momentarily unable to speak over the dry, mealy lump of hurt that formed in her throat. When she was able to go on, she said, "Just because you appreciate my efforts does not mean that . . . others . . . do. I happen to know that your mother is not at all happy with me or my performance in the Wellingham household."

"Surely you jest!" Marc objected, his tone hot with denial. His brows forked and his kind eyes narrowed with scarcely restrained anger. "Has Mother been unkind to you? Has my sister brought up your unfortunate personal circumstances the day I came to your aid on a city street? Has . . . ?"

Feeling the hurt and shame of that incident, Marissa could not face Marc and she turned away. "Well, no. Not to me exactly," she amended. "But one day two weeks ago, I heard your mother confide to one of her social register lady friends that I was lazy, ungrateful, and appallingly lax household help. That she, poor thing, was having to work like a servant herself in order to maintain the mansion properly . . . and that she's considering letting me go. Isabella took up where your mother left off. . . . I won't even repeat the scurrilous things she said."

Marissa's voice cracked on a sob before she could admit to her darling Marc that she'd actually considered resigning and searching for another position. But she couldn't bring herself to do it, for that would mean she could not daily be near the man she loved. And as improbable as it was that Mrs. Wellingham would give her a decent reference, Marissa feared she'd have a difficult time locating another place of employment.

Marissa's quiet snuffles rose to a wail when, instead of clucking in outraged sympathy, Marc laughed. "That clinches it! Now I know for sure that Mother is absolutely *daft* about you, darling!"

Marissa darted him a poisonous look. "You're the one who's daft, Dr. Wellingham. You should have heard the scalding remarks those two made about me. All unfair and untrue, I promise you!"

When Marc's grin remained intact, she glared angrily. "Maybe *you* find this amusing, but I fail to see any humor in it. It's downright hurtful, that's what it is. And humiliating, too, for true." In the throes of her painful litany, Marissa lapsed into her rural dialect. "Why, when I heard your mother sayin' all those nasty things, I got so het up I wanted nothing more than to march right in there and give her a piece of my mind! And Isabella? Well, I fairly itched to scratch her eyes out!" Gaining control of herself somewhat, she attempted to modulate her voice. "Thank the good Lord, I didn't give in to such base behavior, for the gossip would have rendered me unemployable as domestic help from the shores of Lake Michigan to the Iowa border!"

Marc laid a gentle hand on Marissa's hot cheek. "You, my dear, do not know and understand my mother and sister as I do. I've had years and years of experience. My mother is a sly and shrewd woman, the grand mistress of subterfuge, and Isabella is her willing proselyte. Believe me, my sweet, what Mother says is frequently not what she means. I've adjusted to her wily ways over the years. Perhaps that's why I'm so smitten with you. You're guilty of none of those feminine wiles. Generally you're as direct as any gent I've encountered. And I, for one, appreciate knowing exactly where I stand with you."

Marissa remained glum. "I doubt that your mother appreciates that trait in me, either."

"Listen to me, Marissa. Long ago, when I was a wee tad in knee britches, Mother developed a personal code of social conduct that covered her dealings with both her household staff and those she considers her intimates. It was behavior that arose out of her need to protect herself and her interests by controlling and manipulating others, while seemingly allowing them to make their own choices."

"I–I'm afraid I don't understand."

"Mother once learned a very painful lesson, and it's one she's never forgotten. She had a maid who was the epitome of what domestic help should be. She met every one of Mother's very high and exacting standards. Mother was charmed by this woman. Indeed, she was so proud to have such a person in her employ—while her closest friends were lamenting their own sad fortune with household help—that Mother couldn't resist feeling a bit smug and superior. Therefore, she raved on and on, praising the woman's sterling qualities."

"Really?" Marissa breathed, a bit amazed when she compared that long-ago maid's lot with her own circumstances.

Marc nodded. "Yes, and the next thing Mother knew, her cherished maid had given notice. She'd been wooed away by one of Mother's friends, who offered her significantly more pay, in addition to a bonus and shorter hours for agreeing to abandon the Wellingham family and go to work two blocks up the street."

It was an interesting story, but Marissa didn't see what it had to do with her. "So?"

"Don't you see, darling? Mother's a crafty woman. She's merely protecting her interests. She didn't intentionally hurt your feelings. No doubt she never dreamed you overheard the conversation."

"Oh . . . well . . . maybe . . ." Marissa conceded as she processed this new information.

Marc rushed on. "To me, such malicious behavior is proof positive that she doesn't want to risk losing you. So, as usual, she's doing her level best to ensure that it won't happen. By criticizing you, she's guaranteeing that she'll have your services forever! For if her social-register friends think you're a laggard instead of the competent and very talented young woman you are, they won't be working behind her back to beguile you away from us."

Marissa shook her head with amazement. "I must admit, Marc, I hadn't thought of that. But it seems understandable . . . now that you put it that way."

Marc couldn't help grinning. "Beware, however, if Mother should start bragging about you, Marissa, for that means you'll be gone in no time . . . spirited away by some acquaintance of my mother."

Marissa hesitated, then began, "Pardon me if I was overly frank, Marc. I know your mother is a socially prominent woman, educated in the best finishing schools, and that your late father was a much respected businessman. And after your mother opened her home to me . . . well . . . you must think me dreadfully ungrateful."

"'Tis not *her* home, my dear," Marc corrected her. "The mansion belongs to me. We'll live here only as long as I choose. According to the terms of father's will, maintaining or disposing of the family compound is left solely to my discretion. I'm his only son."

"Well, no matter," Marissa said, intent on making her feelings clear, "I'm relieved . . . thankful . . . that you're not at all like your mother."

Marc cocked his head and his grin widened. "Actually, Marissa, I'm a great deal like my mother," he said in a blithe tone. "That is, if I can believe what people have said."

Marissa considered the woman and her son. "They're wrong then," she declared, allowing Marc to draw her into his arms and steal a kiss. She lowered her head to his chest, content to listen to the steady, solid rhythm of his loyal and loving heart. "So very, very wrong."

Marc gave a deep chuckle. "No, you're the one who is in error, my sweet," he corrected. "Adelaide Wellingham is not my mother. She's merely the social-climbing woman who snared my father and became his second wife. She was never a mother to me. She ignored me, thank God, content to entrust me to the care of a loving, Christian woman who was my nanny, so as not to disrupt her social pursuits."

"Marc, I'm amazed! She seems so proud of you. As proud as any mother could be of her natural-born son."

He shrugged it off. "In her own way, perhaps. I suppose I reflect well upon her, for I've been groomed for my place as a physician to Chicago's rich and prosperous. Mother's not so proud to lay claim to *me*, however, as she is prideful of my *profession*. From it, she garners some reflected glory, as if somehow my value gives her additional worth. Oh, she's proud of my accomplishments and lavishly praises me when it suits her. But I have far different desires from those grand plans of Mother's. And my plans, Marissa, include you."

Those were the words Marissa had daydreamed about hearing one day, and that sweet moment was now. "Oh, Marc . . ."

"I can only hope that you love me enough, Marissa, that your plans include me, even if I never become a physician to the wealthy and powerful, with a lucrative big-city practice, treating members of the social register for apoplexy, gout, sour stomach, and flatulence from too many over-indulgences."

Marissa looked at him with eyes shining with love. "I'd adore you no matter what you were," she declared passionately.

"Good! For there are plans afoot, dear girl, that I shan't talk about right now. But it looks as if I . . . we . . . might go far, far away, to an area where I'm desperately needed. A place where I can live up to my Hippocratic Oath as a physician, and more importantly, as a Christian."

"Where you go, Dr. Wellingham, there, too, shall I go," Marissa promised, and meant every word.

chapter

11

MOLLY'S FIRST DAYS in Minnesota were busy, and at times, painful. Time and time again the confrontation with Luke Masterson replayed itself in her mind, and she suffered anew a mortifying swirl of emotions.

In such a small town, she knew that it was only a matter of time before she would be forced to face Luke again, and the very idea of such an encounter caused her stomach to knot up to such a degree that food was not appealing, no matter how effective Rose Grant's culinary efforts.

"You need to eat! You're goin' to waste away to nothin'!" Rose scolded when she realized that Molly was not relishing her good cooking as much as she had a few days earlier.

"I'm fine, really," Molly insisted. "I'm just not hungry. Don't worry about me, Rose. I've plenty to spare. I won't disappear before your eyes."

"See that you don't!" Rose warned good-naturedly. "In just these few days, I've already gotten used to havin' you around and find I rely on you so's my lot would be even worse if suddenly you weren't here."

Molly had worked hard, and Rose understood Molly's need for time to attend to her own interests. So it came as no surprise to her when Molly inquired about a personal concern one morning as they lingered over coffee in the kitchen. "Do you think they'll have clay flowerpots at the mercantile?"

Rose studied Molly over her coffee cup. "I don't know, but you can ask. Why?"

"I brought some rose starts from the graves of my loved ones in Illinois, and I really do need to repot them and set them on the window ledge in my room, or they're going to die."

"We have some old clay pots out in the shed behind the hotel," Rose offered. "They're not fancy, but you're welcome to 'em. It'll save you spendin' your hard-earned money on something you might not be able to afford right now."

"Thank you kindly, Rose. I think I'll tend to the roses during my break this afternoon, for it's a lovely day to be outside," Molly said, glancing out the window and observing the cloudless sky.

"We have a small garden plot out back. I'm sure you've noticed it," Rose said. "Help yourself to some dirt. There's a spade in the shed."

Molly flashed the woman a grateful smile. "I'd been wondering where I could get some topsoil. I'd figured I'd have to walk all the way to the edge of town, and I don't mind telling you that I'd rather dreaded the walk."

Rose squinted her an appraising look. "Your leg's been troublin' you, hasn't it, dear?"

Molly nodded. "A little. I try to ignore it."

"We all try to ignore the things that bother us, don't we?" Rose said reflectively. "Pretend to ourselves they don't exist. But that doesn't make 'em go away."

"That's true enough."

"There's nothing that can be done about your leg?" Rose asked gently.

"I really don't know," Molly admitted. "After the accident, I healed up well enough to get around, so I haven't sought the services of a doctor since. It's a trial I've learned to live with."

"Mayhap if Mr. Masterson is successful in his bid to get a sawbones to settle in these parts, you can consult with him. Or . . ." Rose frowned in thought, "there's even a chance something could be done about your shoes."

"My shoes?"

Rose told Molly the story of a young fellow, born with a clubfoot, whose parents had had the town cobbler create a special pair of shoes to help the child walk more normally.

"Maybe someday," Molly said, then rising, she quickly changed the subject. "But right now, I have to attend to the roses."

"Folks need nurturin' the same as plants and flowers," Rose said soberly. "You need to take care of yourself, Molly, 'specially with you bein' a woman alone. And you've got to let other folks help you. If it's the money that's stoppin' you from consultin' the cobbler, I can advance you the funds."

"Oh, Rose . . ." breathed Molly, overwhelmed by the older woman's generosity.

"You have to surround the rose roots with good dirt, water 'em, give 'em sunlight, maybe even some compost and a road apple or two. But folks are like that, too. We need a fertile environment so's our bodies and spirits can grow. And we need the sunshine of friendship to warm us. My! I reckon I'm gettin' a mite philosophical in my old age," Rose said, chuckling. Her hand slipped to her abdomen. "Must be because of the comin' babe. I find myself thinkin' long thoughts these days."

"Are you overly worried?" Molly asked, sitting back down in her chair.

Rose frowned, taking a while before she answered. "Maybe

a wee bit." Her eyes flicked up to meet Molly's steady gaze. "Actually, a *lot*. I already have seven young'uns, and God forgive me . . . but I wasn't overjoyed to find myself in the family way again. I know that sounds ungrateful to the One who gives life . . . but Molly, I'm tired. So very tired."

"It's not easy, I'm sure," Molly murmured sympathetically.

"Truth to tell, it's a heavy load to carry with my feelin's alone, but it's Albert who's takin' on something awful. He's been saying nasty and hurtful things to me in the privacy of our quarters. Most folks don't know what I live with on a daily basis, and I'm not about to admit it to just anyone," she finished in a whisper.

"I'm so sorry, Rose. Is there anything I can do?"

"You're already doin' it," the older woman said, smiling through her tears. "You're givin' me the sunshine of your friendship, Molly. Without that, I'd probably feel like I was goin' to wither up and die for sure. Hope nothing ever happens to mar our friendship."

"And why should it?" said Molly stoutly, believing that it would be impossible to break the cords they had forged between them.

"Well, just to be on the safe side, I'm lettin' Bert think you're just a regular employee," Rose confessed. "Don't want him to know what good friends we've turned out to be. I–I have to be careful. I know he doesn't love me like he should, but even so, he's jealous. It's like he can't stand the thought of me givin' any of my time to other folks—the young'uns, a woman friend—'cause it takes away from him."

"How awful . . ." Molly was unsure how to comfort her friend.

"Worse than that. . . the man is actually resentful of my relationship with the good Lord!"

140

Molly stared, at a loss for words. The idea was disturbing.

"Albert knew I was a believer when I became his mail-order bride. Guess he figured on takin' it out of me, same as I thought I could help him—an unbeliever—see the need for salvation."

Molly nodded in understanding.

"But it hasn't happened that way, girl," Rose admitted sadly. "Instead, we're unevenly yoked. Lately, seems like my faith ebbs and flows. It's not easy for a Christian to live with an unbeliever. For instance, on Sunday mornin' when I'm rushin' around so's not to be late for the service, he's always findin' some last-minute chore that can't wait for my attention. Probably hopes I'll give up and stop goin' altogether. Then, I want to be able to give more to the church when they pass the collection plate, so's the funds can work to spread the gospel and help those less fortunate. But Albert usually finds somethin' around here we've got to have that money for."

Rose gave a deep sigh and continued. "And the young'uns . . . I'm trying to raise them up in the ways of the Lord. Bert doesn't pester me overly much about the girls—has little use for females, anyway, 'cept at nighttime behind closed doors, when he has his carnal needs to satisfy. But he's givin' me grief about the boys when I try to teach 'em how to be godly Christian men who'll treat a woman right, lovin' her like a part of himself. I feel so torn . . . ," Rose finished at last, her voice trailing off in a wretched whisper.

"It breaks my heart to see you suffer so," Molly said. "For days now, I've been feeling sorry for myself because Luke Masterson rejected me. I guess I was intent on getting married, with or without God's blessing." She looked off through the window once more, feeling remorseful.

"Yes, and when we set our feet to a willful path, it may take a hard blow to get us to turn around," Rose said with the wisdom of experience. "If only I'd turned my cares over to the Lord and trusted him more when I was your age, Molly, I'd be better off now. But I got trapped in worldly snares for awhile, controlled by a father an awful lot like my Bert . . . and I've paid the price every day of my life since."

"Oh . . . Rose . . ." Molly's eyes were wide.

"I do take comfort, though, in my belief in the Lord's sovereignty," the woman went on. "Obviously he allowed me to make those choices of my own free will, knowin' that one day he'd bring good out of the bad, so's I'd look back on my life and see it wasn't all a huge mistake."

"It must sadden you to look back."

Rose nodded. "And it scares me to look ahead."

The hotel proprietress arose and cut herself a large piece of cake and one for Molly. Molly was tempted but resisted. She gave Rose's beefy shoulder a loving pat as she arose to replace the piece of cake intended for her in the glassed-in display shelf where it would stay fresh until dinnertime.

"Don't you like my cookin' anymore, Molly?" Rose asked plaintively.

"My dear Rose," Molly said, gazing at her friend fondly, "I like your cooking entirely too much! I think you probably qualify as the best cook in all of God's creation. But since I've been with you, I've packed on several additional pounds. The clothes I made for this trip are already getting snug, and I can't afford new ones any time soon."

Rose nodded, and Molly knew that the pregnant woman was thinking of the time in the near future when she, too, must have more ample garments to cover her expanding figure.

"Not only that, but I've noticed that my leg is beginning to trouble me more. It's only a few pounds, I know, but while that seems like a trifling amount, my leg protests when my stomach does not."

"Oh, well, all right," Rose conceded, digging into her own slab of cake, but looking guilty.

Molly took a deep breath. "I felt so bad last week that I was willing to do anything to feel better. But while the food helped for a while, I felt worse about myself in other ways. Gaining weight has made me feel . . . well . . . downright ugly. So I've been watching what I eat this week and, Rose," she said, her tone brightening, "I can already tell a difference! Why, I'm beginning to feel like a new person!"

There was a faraway look in Rose's eyes. "I felt good about myself a long time ago . . . when I was a slim slip of a thing," she confessed, wiping a tear. "But it's been *years* since I liked the way I look. I don't even remember what it's like to truly enjoy life."

"Well, you're still living. It can happen again," Molly said gently.

"But I want food," Rose insisted, her voice small and child-like. "It's the only thing that makes me feel good. You know what I mean, don't you, Molly? You enjoy food, too. How can you bear it, not feelin' free to eat whenever you want and whatever you want?"

"It hasn't been easy," Molly admitted. "But it struck me one day that Christians feed on the Scriptures in order to grow strong spiritually. So, when I'm tempted to eat more than I need, I turn to my Bible. Or I think about some of the verses I learned as a child, and turn them over in my mind. It helps to focus my thoughts on something besides my natural appetite."

"Does it work?" Rose wanted to know, her tone dubious.

Molly shrugged. "So far it's helped. And as my clothes get

looser, I feel stronger to resist . . . even when we're working together in the kitchen, preparing delicious dishes for the hotel guests."

"Maybe it would work for me," Rose said hopefully.

"It's worth a try."

Rose looked worried. "I really should do something," she said and fell silent for a long moment.

Molly waited, sensing that Rose had something on her mind and that the woman was wrestling with a decision to unburden herself.

She spoke at last. "I'm scared about this comin' babe, Molly," Rose admitted. "I had a terrible time of it with our last young'un. I thought I was going to die. I was swoll up like a toad by the time my period of travail came. The midwife told me that she'd heard tell that for every pound a woman gained, she'd spend another hour strugglin' to bring her wee one into the world."

"And . . . ?"

"Well, judgin' from the difficult time I had of it, Molly, she was right. I didn't take off the weight after our last one. So I'm still carrying all that and what's come on since. My ankles are already gettin' puffy, and my wedding band's cutting into my finger."

"Maybe we could help each other," Molly suggested. "It's not easy for me, Rose, and I know it would be a chore for you. But when you're weak, then I'll pray the Lord will help me be strong. And when I'm riddled with temptation, then you can come to my aid."

"Well . . . I guess we can try," said Rose doubtfully.

"The Lord doesn't expect more than that."

Rose brightened. "With his help, maybe it'll work, after all."

"Now that that's settled, I'd best get on with repotting the rose shoots," Molly said, getting to her feet once more. "It'll be pleasant to be outside in the fresh air and sunshine. It's easier when I'm not in the kitchen between meals, taking a moment of ease."

"Speaking of our leisure," Rose spoke up, "we won't have many more such moments before winter sets in. And, I vow and declare, girl, you've never seen winters like we have in these parts."

Molly shivered. "It makes me cold just to think of it."

"I've about given up hope of us havin' our own physician before the new year," Rose lamented. "Or a pastor in time for Christmas worship services."

"Then we'll just have to keep praying."

"There *is* hope," Rose said, "as long as Luke Masterson is workin' on it."

Molly felt a little uncomfortable at the mention of Luke's name. "I'm glad to hear that."

"Well, I'm goin' to do more than *hope*," declared Rose with sudden determination. "He's about due to come here for dinner, and when he does, I'm goin' to ask him about the rumors I've heard of a business trip to Minneapolis-St. Paul, or maybe it was Chicago . . . to search for a man of the cloth and a doctor for our town. If it's true, then I want to urge him on and thank him, too."

At the thought of facing Luke Masterson, Molly felt herself quail. "I just hope I'm not on duty when he arrives," she blurted out. "And if I am, would you please fill in for me, Rose, so I don't have to serve him?"

Rose nodded reluctantly. "But you can't run away forever, Molly. Somehow you'll find a way to handle a meetin' between the two of you, for it's goin' to happen, sooner or later. Trust the Lord to give you the grace to see it through.

"Mayhap Luke Masterson doesn't want you . . . or any woman . . . for a wife. But that doesn't mean he's dead set against havin' you as a cordial acquaintance in the town where you both reside. And who knows? Someday you may even be friends."

"Humph! That's hardly likely," Molly murmured.

"But with the Lord, anything is possible, isn't that so?" Rose lumbered to her feet and deposited the half-eaten slice of cake in the slop bucket. "Why, I'm even hopeful I can become a slim slip of a thing again. Oh, if those days could only return!"

"They can," Molly assured her, patting her friend on the arm.

Rose sighed. "I've always believed that if I could be slim, things would be right, I'd be truly happy, and my husband would love me like he should. But now that I've been turnin' it over in my mind, I'm thinkin' I've got it all backward." Her expression took on an exalted look as an idea dawned. "Maybe . . . if I can find reasons to be happy with my lot . . . then I won't bury myself in my good cookin' and I'll really find my life again."

chapter
12

To Molly's relief, over the next few weeks, when Luke Masterson came to the Grant Hotel to dine, Rose was as good as her word and left her labors in the kitchen to take over in the dining room. On those occasions, Molly quietly slipped back to the kitchen and worked feverishly so Rose wouldn't regret the temporary exchange of duties.

In the two months since Molly and Luke had had their first encounter, Molly had lost twenty pounds. So it was not the same young woman who appeared to wait on him when he arrived at the hotel dining room early one winter evening.

This time, Molly had no recourse but to wait on him, for Rose had fallen ill in the late afternoon, suffering spasms that radiated across her back and abdomen. A worried Molly had insisted that the woman take to her bed and leave all the kitchen duties to herself and young Becky Grant.

Throughout the evening, Molly had explained to patrons that Rose was not well and had found them to be completely understanding and lavish in their praise of the tasty meal. And when at last, Molly was beginning to see an end to the endless stream of customers, Luke Masterson appeared, almost exactly at closing time.

Molly, whose limp had grown steadily more pronounced due to fatigue during the long evening, was tempted to send Becky to tell him that the dining room was closed. But when she saw him shiver and cross to the hearth in the lobby to warm himself, she didn't have the heart to send him away cold and hungry, no matter what their past experience.

Pretending that the horrible confrontation had never taken place, Molly swept in from the kitchen, trying to control her limp. "Good evening, sir," she said in a pleasant voice, which thankfully seemed to reveal none of the nervousness she felt. "We have a nice table over here in the corner where it's warm from the kitchen."

"Fine," he said, and slipped off his heavy overcoat, placing it on the oak hall tree. "You're looking very well, Miss Wheeler."

"Why, thank you," she said, flushing with appreciation at the unexpected compliment. Slim as she now was, she sensed that the judgment was true and relished the fact that he had noticed.

Luke followed Molly to the table, seated himself, then listened intently as she rattled off the evening menu, along with the remaining dessert selections.

With little rumination, making Molly believe that here was a man who knew what he wanted and went right after it, he quickly gave his order.

"Coffee while you wait?"

"Yes, thanks."

"With cream?"

"Black, please."

Molly made her way back to the kitchen. Earlier, she had planned to have Becky take Mr. Masterson's plate to him when the order was complete, but as pleasant as he'd been to her, she decided to serve him herself. Perhaps facing him now would make any future encounters less unnerving.

He was acting as if he either didn't remember her, or had long since forgotten their unfortunate beginnings. Had he truly put it from his mind, or was he playing some kind of game? Molly felt like a frightened rabbit caught behind the bead of a hunter's rifle.

The mystery was soon solved, for when she returned to refill his cup, he spoke again. "You've been avoiding me," Luke accused lightly, in a tone that somehow did not seem judgmental.

Molly felt herself grow pale. "And what if I have? Certainly you've been no more eager to see me than I have been to see you!" The retort leapt to her lips before she could censor herself.

"Actually, that's where you're wrong, Miss Wheeler. For I've been hoping to see you and apologize for my unforgivable behavior the day you came to my office. It just happened that your arrival was simply the straw that broke the camel's back after the drunken melee I had been refereeing at the lumber camp that day."

"Oh, no apologies necessary," Molly said crisply, wishing only to drop the topic, for while the memory had faded, more residue of pain still remained than she had realized.

"I insist that an apology is in order, Miss Wheeler," Luke insisted, "for I was a thoughtless cad at best. Many times I've tried to pen a note expressing my regret over what happened, but somehow the words never came out right. And I wasn't sure you'd even open a note from me. So I've bided my time in the hope that you'd hear me out if I appeared in person."

"I see."

"I had no right to say those cruel things to you—," he flinched at the memory, "assigning to you questionable motives. Clearly, I couldn't have been more wrong in my suppositions."

"You were rather flustered at the moment, I recall," Molly

murmured with the beginning of a twinkle in her eye. "And I was unduly tense myself. It was an unfortunate situation all the way around, for we both found ourselves victims of a cruel hoax."

"Then I'm forgiven my boorish behavior?"

Molly nodded. "Of course . . . if you'll forgive me the heartless comments I flung in your direction."

"Done . . . and long ago at that," Luke agreed affably. "But what hasn't been done is to find a suitable punishment for the lumberjacks who perpetrated this crime against us. I've isolated the rascals involved, and they remain in the firm's employ, though they're aware that they must offer up some kind of restitution for the pain inflicted. To date, however, I haven't conceived the perfect atonement. They're good loggers and if the penalty is too high, they'll move on to work for a competitor. But if they get off with only a slap on the wrist, I fear they'll have no compunction about repeating the stunt."

"Give it time . . . and prayer," Molly encouraged him. "The Lord will help you find the right answer and guide you in how best to proceed."

Luke leveled a long look. "You really believe that, don't you?"

It seemed clear to Molly that as a timber boss, accustomed to making decisions, issuing orders, and having them followed to the letter, the idea of placing his destiny in other hands than his was foreign to Luke Masterson. It was frightening to Molly that he felt no need to consult the Divine Creator who reigns over all, be they power brokers or the most humble.

But her reply was firm. "Absolutely. Indeed," she confided, "I now think I understand why I was brought to these parts.

I came with the intention of marrying, but instead, I found myself exactly where the Lord wanted me—in the abode of Rose Grant, a good and godly woman who needs me right now."

Luke frowned. "Rose doesn't look well, hasn't for the last fortnight, now that I think of it. Robust woman that she is, she appears peaked to me."

"She's confined to her quarters this evening," Molly admitted. "I'm afraid she's not doing at all well."

"Nothing serious, I hope? There's been some grippe going around, and it seems someone is always suffering with consumption."

An uncomfortable silence spiraled between them.

"Just a common . . . malady . . . that will ease sometime in the coming year," Molly replied, feeling her cheeks flush hotly and hoping she'd chosen an appropriately delicate manner in which to impart such news to a gentleman. "Now I'd best get back to the kitchen. I'm sure your dinner is ready by now."

Luke glanced around the dining room, deserted now save for the two of them. "Might you have a moment to linger over a cup of coffee or a spot of tea and keep me company? I'd appreciate it, although I know you're a busy woman. And our past being what it is, I'd understand if you chose not to spend another second in conversation with me."

"I . . . I think I can spare some time. It will feel good to get off my feet," Molly admitted, then felt like kicking herself for drawing his attention to her limp, as if the man hadn't eyes in his head!

Becky had dished up Luke's order—hearty portions—and the plate looked attractive as Molly carried it to the table, placed a small basket of warm dinner rolls nearby, then returned to the kitchen for a clean cup and carried the pot of coffee back to the table, setting it on a trivet.

Suddenly words did not come easy, so Molly busied herself pouring the coffee as Luke prepared to dine. She noticed that he neatly unfolded the linen napkin, smoothed it into place, and then maintained good posture as he ate, using what Molly considered flawless manners.

Watching Rose Grant's Albert bolt down his food morning, noon, and night, hunched over the work table, eating with the manners of a wild boar, caused Molly to appreciate even more the etiquette of a refined man like Luke Masterson.

"More coffee, Mr. Masterson?" She lifted the pot inquiringly before pouring herself another cup of the steaming brew that had miraculously revived her senses.

"I don't mind if I do." He nudged the cup toward her. "But please . . . call me Luke."

She had been hoping for just such a suggestion. "If you'll call me Molly."

"With pleasure, Molly. And how do you find it here in our fledgling town? It must be very different from where you hail from . . . Illinois, I believe?"

Molly nodded.

"I'll be traveling to Chicago within the fortnight," he said. "But I recall that you came from some other town, is that right?"

Molly found herself telling him all about Effingham, Watson, and the Salt Creek community in particular. She hadn't realized how homesick she was for those dear people and places until she began to reminisce with a willing listener. "Yes, it's very different from my home," she finished. "But I think I'll like it here, though I'm unsure just how long I'll stay. At present I have no immediate plans to leave, but I'll have to say that although I lived in the country, I'm accustomed to living near larger towns with more services than Williams has to offer."

Luke frowned. "There are a group of us—local citizens I've rallied around the cause—who are working zealously to rectify some of Williams's shortcomings, two of them being the unavailabilty of a doctor and a pastor for the local church."

"I truly hope you'll be successful, for I'm sure the entire town would benefit."

"We're doing our best," Luke assured her, "and spending no small amount of time and our own funds in an effort to bring some good people to this region. I'll be leaving soon to continue the search." He edged away from the table and deposited his used linen—and a coin of gratuity—on the tablecloth. "But I doubt I'll have such a fine meal again until I return."

"Mrs. Grant's an exemplary cook," Molly murmured, taking none of the credit for herself.

"Wonderful woman, too," Luke Masterson agreed. "I'm sorry to learn that she's feeling poorly this evening."

Molly, unsure of the propriety of a maiden continuing to discuss a pregnant matron's health with a single gentleman, hesitated. "She's . . . a bit under the weather, more so than usual. She hasn't felt fit since we first became acquainted, actually. I've tried to urge her to pay a call on the . . . local midwife . . . but Rose is a busy woman and she tends to put her own needs to the hind."

"Would that be Mrs. Woolery? Archie's wife?"

"I really don't know. She hasn't mentioned her by name."

"There aren't many midwives in Williams," Luke explained. "Archie is one of my best cutters. Perhaps when I venture out to the logging camp he's assigned to, tomorrow or the next day, I'll ask him to tell his wife that Rose isn't feeling well. There is sure to be some herb or other preparation to ease her miseries."

In the face of the man's tender concern, Molly threw caution to the winds. "I'd be ever so grateful if you would, Luke! Rose has confided some of her woes to me, but it's an area of which I have no real knowledge. But from what she's described to me, and from the pain I see on her face, I've been dreadfully worried about her."

"She's not a young woman anymore," Luke said. "And she's a little . . . heavier . . . than she ought to be."

"Yes, and she fears that will cause her added grief . . . later on. Rose and I are concerned that a midwife's expertise may not be enough this time. We're praying that Williams will have a physician to attend her when her time comes."

"When is the happy event?" Luke asked delicately. "So I can keep the date forefront in my mind when I interview physicians."

The question hung between them.

Molly glanced away. "She hasn't said, exactly, but from my calculations, I'd say late winter or early spring."

"God willing, we'll have a doctor in town by then," Luke promised. "But in the meantime, the admonitions of a midwife will have to suffice."

"Rest assured, I'm going to insist on taking on more of Rose's chores until . . . she's herself again," Molly declared. "And Becky will help. She's showing signs of being as competent as her mother."

"Mrs. Grant has always worked entirely too hard, in my estimation," Luke observed with a bitter laugh. "If only her husband were half as industrious. Most days it seems the bloke scarcely turns a tap except to flip a card at the Black Diamond Saloon, or adjourn to his accustomed seat on the Liars' Bench and puff his pipe. No doubt the man hasn't taken into account that, if he doesn't come to his wife's aid, he may find himself alone with seven children, perhaps an eighth, if Rose should die in the birthing."

Luke's handsome features twisted in an expression of disgust. "Of course, should that happen, God forbid, Bert would probably take no more responsibility for the family's welfare than he has while she's living. I, for one, wouldn't be surprised if he didn't pack them all up like a litter of unwanted kittens and deposit them on the doorstep of the nearest orphanage in the dark of night!"

"The situation is that dire?" Molly whispered as fear clutched her heart.

She didn't know Albert Grant well, but she'd been around him enough to realize that she didn't like him, though she'd tried to give him the benefit of the doubt for Rose's sake. But suddenly she sensed that it was exactly as Luke had intimated. Rose Grant's family circumstances were grim indeed.

Molly knew Rose wasn't a complainer, but it was now clear that for every startling admission the woman had made, there were probably ten others she had kept to herself. Molly suspected that her friend only unburdened herself fully to the Lord, hoping others would not be able to detect the worsening condition in which she found herself.

"That dire," Luke replied, nodding quietly. "And something must be done about it. But the approach can't be obvious. It must be rather . . . covert. You're a church-going woman, aren't you, Molly?" he asked appearing to change the subject.

Molly gave Luke a puzzled look, recalling what Rose had

said about his infrequent church attendance. "Yes. Why do you ask?"

He regarded her steadily across the table. It was clear that his mind was swirling with possibilities for improving Rose's condition. "At risk of sounding forward, I wonder if you would mind if I began coming by on Sunday mornings with a wagon, weather permitting, or a cutter when there's snow on the ground, and transporting you to church."

Molly was mystified. After weeks of painstakingly avoiding being anywhere in the vicinity of Luke Masterson, the idea of regularly keeping company with him was unsettling. But she didn't want to hurt his feelings, so she sought a reasonable excuse for declining. "Actually, I enjoy the walk," she demurred. "It's brisk and bracing and gives me time to organize my thoughts on the way, meditate a bit, and prepare myself to be fed in faith for the coming week."

Molly clamped her lips shut. There she went again, dithering like a foolish woman! She realized that she had enjoyed knowing they shared a concern for Rose's best interests, enjoyed Luke's seeking her advice. She was beginning to feel more like his ally than his sworn enemy. She certainly didn't want to jeopardize their tenuous relationship now.

"Please don't misunderstand me," Luke said in a whisper, seeming to read the path Molly's thoughts were taking, "I wouldn't want to give you the impression that I was interested in courting you, Miss Wheeler, for that's not the case." His tone was so sincere, his expression so earnest that Molly knew he hadn't been aware of the spear of fresh pain that penetrated to the heart with his words. Then he shrugged. "Although it might not hurt if it appears that way to others."

"I'm not sure what you're driving at, Luke," Molly admitted. "I handled my late pa's workhorses. Perhaps I could . . ."

"I wouldn't hear of it, Molly," Luke interjected. "Besides, the solution is really quite simple. If you'll cooperate with me so it would look to the townspeople as if I were accompanying *you* to worship services, then it would be very natural, wouldn't it, if we'd do the kind thing and invite your employer to ride with us? That's one way we can keep Rose Grant off her feet as much as possible while she awaits her coming child."

Molly couldn't believe her ears. "Oh, that's brilliantly thoughtful of you, Luke! And if Rose thinks you're interested in me, she'll find it easier to accept a ride, for she likes both of us very, very much and it'll settle a lot of things in her heart if she believes the thorny past is behind us."

"And it can be," Luke muttered under his breath. "Do you think Rose will suspect our plans to safeguard her health?"

Molly's sweet face was flushed, her eyes shining with excitement. "I do hope not. She's extremely independent, you know. She likes to do for others, but seems to have trouble when the shoe is on the other foot. But your idea seems the perfect solution."

Luke flashed a dazzling smile. "Then it's settled! I'm glad you're agreeable, Molly. But we'll have to be careful so as not to let the cat out of the bag. Rose must never figure it out and put the kibosh on our scheme."

chapter
13

THE NEXT WEEK-AND-A-HALF was the most enjoyable since Molly's arrival in Williams.

She had received several letters from Lizzie and a number from Katie. Two of them bore her sister's maiden name in the return address—"Mary Katharine Wheeler"—and the most recent, if undeliverable, was to be sent back to "Mrs. Seth Hyatt."

Molly, in turn, had written to both Lizzie and Katie, with various remarks directed to the attention of others in the community. Realizing that any communication from her would be carried in the women's handbags and circulated at gatherings, she had penned her thoughts accordingly.

Since Molly had not confided her plans to become a mail-order bride, she was spared the need to confess that she'd failed in the attempt. It was a relief not to have to admit her humiliation and hurt following her arrival in Minnesota, where she had met with rejection rather than the fulfillment of her most private dreams.

In her letters, Molly described the town of Williams, her job at the hotel, and her continuing hope that one day the area could support a milliner's shop, an enterprise she intended to undertake at some date in the near future. And it was only natural that she should write about the folks who peopled her new life—Rose Grant and her children, the hotel's regular customers, the owner of the mercantile, who also

served as the postmaster. There were also the people she'd
met at the pastorless church, who reminded her so much of
the close-knit congregation in the little church on the banks
of Salt Creek.

Casually, she dropped the mention of her latest acquaintance.

> There's a man, Luke Masterson, a timber boss for Meloney
> Brothers Lumber Company, a business much like Seth operates,
> but on a grander scale, who sometimes dines at the Grant Hotel
> where I work. He has requested that I allow him to escort me
> and Mrs. Grant to worship services on Sunday morning. It is not
> a long walk to the church building, but the cord roads are rough
> with muddy sloughs that are hazardous in inclement weather.

And with that, Molly left the rest to the active imaginations
of the womenfolk in her family. Lizzie, Katie, and the
Mathews girls would no doubt read more into her somewhat
duplicitous words than was intended, though she secretly
hoped they *would* think Luke Masterson was her beau. Lizzie,
who was the only one who knew Molly's true reason for leaving central Illinois, might take comfort in the speculation that
she had found a man of her own to love at last.

> Since leaving Illinois, I have lost twenty pounds. It is my opin-
> ion, and seems to be that of others, that I have never looked bet-
> ter. I do know that somehow I feel more confident and have a
> sense of fitness and well-being. Another appealing aspect is that
> my bad leg troubles me less often, too. So losing weight has been
> a multiplied blessing. These days, when I'm tempted to take a
> generous portion on my plate, instead of satisfying my hunger
> for tasty morsels, I turn to the Good Book for nourishment of
> another kind. And it works! In addition, I feel more prepared
> when I'm asked to lead the Sunday school lessons at our church.

This regimen is working, not only for me but also for dear Rose, a lovely woman who reminds me of your late mother, Fanchon, Lizzie. She is in the family way with her eighth child. Rose is so attractive, so fun-loving, but she is overly large, and I pray she'll know the same success as we tackle our weight problems together, for her health is not as vibrant as it should be.

Luke and I worry about her immediate future, as well, as her husband is of little assistance to her. Williams has no doctor, and we desperately need to find a physician to tend our bodily needs as well as a pastor to shepherd the local flock and help us mature as Christians.

Luke will be leaving for St. Paul, Chicago, and other points in the very near future. His planned trip to Chicago brings Marissa to mind daily. I find my thoughts turning in that direction more and more with every day that passes. As I mentioned in an earlier letter, I searched for her while I was there, but to no avail. I feel so helpless, loving her as I do and wanting what's good for her. I can't let myself dwell on the thought that she might have already departed this life. Believing I'll see my beloved twin again encourages me to have faith. Keeping her in my prayers, as I know you do, makes me feel we're doing something positive, not just consigning her to who knows what dire fortune!

If, by chance, you should hear from 'Rissa, I would appreciate it if you would telegraph the news to me rather than post a missive and risk further delay. I would assume the depot agent here could pass on a telegram to me. I would gladly reimburse you the expense involved since I am now a working girl, making good wages. Living and dining at the hotel, my expenses—except for a tithe in the collection plate at services—are quite few.

I'm tempted, at times, as Mr. Masterson's business trip looms nearer, to ask him to inquire after Marissa while he is in the Windy City. But I stifle the urge, for he might make it his first order of business and neglect the matters that called him from the northland. Missing Sis as I do, I trust in God that we will one day be reunited. If not in this world . . . then in the next.

I have potted the rose starts you gave me, Lizzie. What a generous and thoughtful gesture that was. They are surviving in the clay pots Mrs. Grant donated, but they are not thriving. Winters here are hard, and already I find myself anticipating the coming spring when I'll be able to transplant them in the warm soil. My hope is that they will soon be blooming as prolifically as the bushes from which they sprang. I shall always remember the fragrance when, after a summer rain, the air was so sweet with the scent of roses. . . .

Molly had just completed, signed, and sealed the bulky letter to the folks at home when a glance at her timepiece told her she must end her workbreak and go downstairs to help Rose and Becky prepare and serve the evening meal.

Finding Rose already in the kitchen, Molly was pleased to see that two days of bed rest seemed to have done much to rejuvenate the older woman in both body and spirit. Although Molly urged caution, an eager Rose Grant returned to her labors with gale-force enthusiasm.

That morning Molly had met Mrs. Woolery, the midwife, and was grateful that Luke, true to his word, had intervened. Molly had liked her on sight but had felt dreadfully homesick for dear Lizzie, for although the women bore little physical resemblance to one another, there was something about them that told Molly they had been cut out of the same bolt of cloth.

Letting Rose believe she had just happened by, Mrs. Woolery had graciously accepted an invitation to have coffee and, during the morning, artfully turned the conversation to Rose's health, expressing proper surprise about the impending birth. She was quick to offer suggestions for Rose to follow in ensuring a birth that was as easy on her as possible and would result in a healthy infant.

Upon her departure, Mrs. Woolery had ticked off some patent medicines that Rose needed to help her build her strength for the coming months, and promised to deliver some herbal nostrums of her own creation, as well.

"Rose, dear," she said, laying a hand on the hotel proprietress's shoulder, "I'm so relieved you have someone to help you." The woman turned to Molly. "For I'm sure I'll have a wonderful accomplice in our town's newest resident. She can watchdog you in my stead, right, Molly?"

"Consider it done," Molly promised with a smile.

"See that she takes her rest," Mrs. Woolery had stressed. "And stay away from sweets, Rose. I know what a weakness you have! But it's meat, vegetables, and milk that will knit a strong baby in your womb."

With these cautions in mind, Molly proceeded downstairs to the kitchen, intent on doing more than her fair share in order to spare Rose. While she worked, she found her thoughts pleasantly swirling over possibilities for the evening. She had understood that in the past Luke Masterson was only a sporadic diner at the Grant Hotel. And when he'd appeared three nights earlier, she had believed that it would be the last she'd see of him until their Sunday morning appointment.

But Luke returned the next night . . . and the next, arriving near the end of the posted dinner hours, when the dining room was either deserted or when the few remaining stragglers were about to depart.

Molly made a point of giving Luke expert service, not only to do the hotel proud but because she felt strangely drawn to him. She believed, too, that he appreciated her company, for she sensed, deep down, that even though he was surrounded by employees at the lumber company, Luke Masterson was a lonely man.

"Can you spare a few minutes for a cup of coffee with me again this evening?" he asked, as he had on previous nights, a request that Molly had grown to anticipate.

But when he made the request for the third evening in a row, with Mrs. Woolery's admonitions still fresh in her mind, Molly felt torn. "I'd love to, Luke, but we had more diners tonight than usual, and there are mounds of dirty dishes stacked up in the galley. I wouldn't want the burden of cleaning up to fall on Rose while I'm idling away my time."

"No doubt Rose has been on her feet long enough for one day," he announced brusquely, his jaw firmly flexed. "I'm sure you'd have no objections to her joining us." And without waiting for her reply, he rose.

"Of–of course not," Molly stammered. "It would be a pure pleasure . . . but it'll take a miracle to convince her to leave the kitchen."

Luke's quick grin made Molly's heart turn over, for he seemed more handsome than ever, his eyes all alight and his mustache capping a charming smile over strong teeth that were gleaming white against his deeply tanned face. "One small miracle coming right up."

In another minute or two, he was back with a flustered Rose Grant in tow. "You're a sweet-talker, you are," Rose accused but seemed grateful for the excuse to get off her feet over a steaming cup of tea. "I'm near about to swoon away that you'd have such chivalrous words to spare me when I'd think you'd be saving them to bestow on our Molly-girl here!"

Molly felt her cheeks heat as she realized that her friend was reading into the situation exactly what Luke had intended. The threesome relaxed over their hot beverages, discussing the topics of the day that had made news in the small town.

"This is most enjoyable," Rose said at last, "but my work's a-waitin'. Now don't hurry on my account, Molly. You and Luke must have lots to talk about without an extra ear listenin' in," she said as she got to her feet, swaying unsteadily.

"You're not going to back out on our deal now, are you, Mrs. Grant?" Luke's narrowed eyes flashed dangerously.

"Oh, bosh, young man! I thought you were just jollyin' me along with your bribes to abandon the dishpan and join you and Molly at the table. Little did I know you'd not release me from my agreement when the time came! Besides, a man says a lot of things he doesn't mean when he's courtin'."

"Not this fellow," Luke objected. "My word is my bond, and once I strike a deal there's no going back on it. Now, my dear Mrs. Grant, you agreed to the terms. Surely you're not going to renege, are you?"

"Humph! I should certainly say I am!"

"Come now, my good woman," he said, rising to help her from the table. "Your quarters and a comfortable bed await you."

"But, Mr. Masterson, doin' up dishes is *woman's* work," she insisted. "It's not fittin' . . . you being a guest of the hotel and all."

"As I recall, when I was living at the Orphan's Home," Luke went on quietly, "there was no *woman's* work and *man's* work. There was simply *work* . . . and we attended to it as we saw the need. I'm rather handy with a dishcloth and towel, if I do say so myself. Give me one of your aprons, Rose Grant, and I'll feel right at home. Some of my most enjoyable moments were spent scouring pots and pans when I was a wee lad with no family to claim but the other orphans."

"Can you believe this man?" A flustered Rose turned to Molly for support.

"He's right," said Molly firmly. "If Mr. Masterson doesn't mind, I don't mind."

"Well, I mind!" Rose huffed.

Luke waggled a finger in front of her face. "Two against one. I think you've been outvoted, Rose. Now go along with you and think of the newest member of the Grant family, soon to come. Surely you want better than an orphan's home for him or her, don't you?"

At his words, intended only as lighthearted bantering, Rose's complexion, reddened from steam in the kitchen, blanched as pale as flour. It was something to consider . . . that if something happened to her, her young'uns would doubtless be consigned to a harsh fate by their indifferent father.

"Oh, all right, I'll do it," she grumbled. "But I can't be happy about shirkin' my duties."

"Rest assured that, come the dawn when you arrive to begin preparing breakfast, the kitchen will be spotless and everything in its place . . . and Molly and I will enjoy ourselves in the process."

Reluctantly, but with a certain sly smile, Rose turned toward the Grant family's quarters down the hall from the kitchen and lobby.

Luke bowed from the waist. "Good night, Mrs. Grant. Sleep well." And turning to Molly, he crooked an elbow. "Coming, my dear?"

Laughing lightly, she looped her arm through his. But so dazzled was Molly with the magical moment that she gave no thought to the dishes remaining on the table until she noticed that Luke, with his free hand, had scooped them up and was carrying them into the cluttered kitchen.

"You really don't have to do this, Luke," Molly said when they were alone. "I can attend to the chores myself."

"And don't I know that!" he said admiringly. "But it's my choice." Then giving her no room for argument, he asked, "Do you prefer to wash or dry?"

Molly smiled and shook her head helplessly. "You're the guest . . . you choose."

"Then I'll wash," he decided. "But I'll have to trouble you for an apron."

Molly retrieved a fresh apron from the cupboard and handed it to Luke. He slipped it on but fumbled so with the straps and closures that she was eventually forced to help him tie it.

"There," she said as she tied the bow and then hastily moved away to draw hot water from the reservoir in the wood range.

Talk between them came easily, and almost too soon it seemed, the cabinet and sideboard that had been piled high with used utensils, plates, bowls, pots and pans, were swept clear and the clean items stowed in their assigned shelves.

Removing the voluminous apron, Luke handed it to Molly. "It's been a memorable evening. Now I must move along so you can retire. Morning comes early, and I'm sure this has been as long a day for you as for Rose."

"I've enjoyed it, too," Molly admitted, trailing in Luke's wake as he crossed to the hall tree to collect his coat.

"Perhaps we can inveigle Mrs. Grant into an encore tomorrow evening."

"You'll be returning then," Molly murmured, surprised.

"You can count on it . . . until I'm called away on business."

"I'll look forward to it." Molly was hard put to believe she would be favored by Luke Masterson's presence on a regular basis, but despite his ulterior motives, she intended to savor every moment.

At the door, Luke seemed to hesitate. He regarded Molly steadily, turning something over and over in his mind. Then, most unexpectedly and before she could think or react, he bent his head and brushed her cheek with his lips. "Stay sweet," he ordered.

And then he was gone.

Molly would have believed that the thrilling interlude was a figment of her imagination were it not for the fact that she could still feel the warm imprint of his lips on her cheek, the titillating texture of his mustache on her soft skin.

She shivered with the blast of wintry wind that blew in with Luke's departure. As she watched him leave, all she could think was that he had promised to be back the following evening. And Luke Masterson was a man of his word.

So she squelched the knowledge that he was doing all this for the sake of a tired, overworked woman who was in the family way and not because he was smitten with Molly Wheeler. It didn't matter. For Molly was hopelessly in love with a man who had vowed never to marry.

chapter
14

DESPITE HER BEST intentions, Molly found herself counting the hours until dinnertime each evening. And Luke didn't disappoint her. Each night, not long before the hotel dining room's official closing time, he appeared.

Rose Grant, believing she was allowing a courting couple time in which to enjoy one another's company, gratefully acquiesced when they urged her to take her ease and departed for her own quarters, leaving them alone to take care of the kitchen chores.

Molly had observed that she and Luke made a good pair, alternating between washing and drying duties and keeping each other amused with tales of their past and tidbits of gossip that circulated through the town. In Luke's company, the time fairly flew and the task was accomplished in record time. And each evening, when Luke donned his greatcoat and took his leave, she was vaguely disconcerted and retired to the privacy of her room, feeling more bereft than ever.

Saturday evening was no exception. Luke showed up at the expected hour, but Molly noticed that when they finished their kitchen duties, he seemed in no hurry to depart and this emboldened her. "There's a bit of coffee in the pot," she said. "Would you have one last cup before you leave? There's a nice blaze in the fireplace in the lobby."

Luke hesitated only the length of time between one heartbeat and the next. "I don't mind if I do."

"You could place another chunk of wood on the fire if you like," Molly suggested. "It does make the room cheerful."

He obliged while Molly prepared a tray with two cups of coffee and several dainty sugar cookies she had baked that afternoon, using Lizzie Mathew's recipe, the one that had won awards at the Watson Town Fair. Then she carried the tray to the lobby and positioned it on a table as Luke drew up two wingback chairs closer to the fire.

They sat in silence for a few moments, savoring the hot coffee and the warmth of the hearth. And when Luke began to share plans for his upcoming trip, with details of his itinerary, Molly realized that she had never been happier in her entire life. She was startled, then disappointed when the grandfather clock in the corner struck eleven.

Luke got to his feet. "I really must be going. I had no idea the hour was so late," he said. "I'm keeping you from your rest."

"Oh, that's quite all right," Molly said sincerely, even though in recent moments she'd been stifling random yawns.

"We *both* have to arise early tomorrow. I may have neglected to tell you," Luke said, "but I plan to stay for the service tomorrow, though I rarely attend church. Still, it occurred to me that Mrs. Grant might suspect something is amiss if I rather ungallantly deposit you at the church door."

Molly felt a moment's hurt. All week long she'd believed that Luke was now spending time with her because he enjoyed her company. But nothing had changed. It was still only part and parcel of a carefully planned ruse by a businessman who was adept at keeping up appearances.

"I'm sure you'll enjoy the services," Molly said, trying to conceal her disappointment. "Even without a parson, they're actually quite edifying."

"I'll warm a pew, but I trust no one will expect me to take an active part." For a moment, Luke's voice took on an obstinate quality.

Molly shrugged. "Not unless you're moved to."

"We had some religious malarkey forced upon us at the Orphan's Home. Some took to it like ducks to water. I, alas, was not among that number. I've always been too much of a free-thinker to simply follow the masses blindly."

"We're hardly 'the masses,'" Molly said, stung by his implication. "I consider myself a part of the mystical body of Christ, the Church, but each believer is different from every other believer, Luke, even though we're united in our common faith in Jesus as our personal Savior and Lord. But each and every one of us has our own talents, strengths . . . weaknesses, too, I fear," she admitted. "And our stories of faith are as diverse as we are."

"I've a friend who would certainly agree with what you're saying, Molly. Perhaps someday you'll meet the man."

"I'd like that very much."

"God willing, Molly," Luke went on, "he'll be the new pastor . . . if I can negotiate a deal to get him to accept the call to the Williams church."

"I'll be praying you're successful," Molly murmured.

"Go ahead and pray," Luke agreed, but there was a touch of cynicism in his tone. "Then hope that I can convince him to relocate to what even a man of God might deem a godforsaken wilderness!"

"I'll mention it in my prayers tonight," Molly said as she arose and crossed to the coat tree.

Luke took down his garment and shrugged into it. Unable to help herself, Molly stood on tiptoe and smoothed the collar on his broad shoulders, then deftly tucked the woolen scarf in at his throat. "There! Now you're ready for the bitter cold."

Luke looked at her with a strange light in his eyes. A look that both thrilled and terrified her. He said not a word, but kept his gaze riveted on her, as if seeing her for the first time. "Oh, Molly," he whispered softly. "Molly . . ." This time her name was a faint groan, and then he was drawing her to him.

There was no time to prepare for Luke's gentle touch on her face, his forefinger stroking the sleek line where, only three months before, there had been excess flesh at the jowl. Now her fine facial bone structure, which made her more resemble her pretty mother, was revealed.

Molly opened her mouth to speak his name, first in surprise, and then questioningly. But he halted further speech with the soft pressure of his lips on hers, lightly, then in a lingering kiss.

Molly felt weak, almost woozy, and was grateful when Luke's arms tightened around her, thrilling with the knowledge that there was so much less of her to embrace than when they'd met a few months before. She knew that she hadn't been unattractive then, but she was aware that she cut a much more appealing figure now, a fact that had not escaped Luke's notice.

Her heart sang when his lips claimed hers once more, believing that Luke was with her because he wanted to be, not just to safeguard Rose Grant's health. And she believed— had to believe with all of her heart—that Luke's plans to attend church with her were not just for the sake of appearance, but because the Lord was calling to him . . . and Luke Masterson's once-hard heart was softening.

"I'll see you in the morning," Luke whispered, seeming no

less affected by the force of their chaste intimacies than Molly. "Sleep well."

"And you," Molly whispered back. "Goodnight . . ."

When he was gone, Molly felt as if somehow a part of him had remained, even as she realized that he'd taken with him, an even larger part of her heart.

Molly scarcely slept that night for the almost giddy thoughts that spun through her brain. Even so, she awoke with enthusiasm, hastily preparing herself, primping over her hair, intent on looking her best when Luke came to call. How proud she would be to have him sitting beside her at church!

Rose Grant, too, was beaming as Molly waited in the lobby for Luke to arrive. Molly had already confided to her that Luke was coming to collect her for services, pointing out how useless it would be for Rose to walk to church when Luke and Molly would be going there shortly. "There's room for the children, too," Molly had stressed.

"I thank you kindly, and don't mind if I do," Rose had said, "though I hope you sparkin' young'uns won't mind having my old bones along."

"Don't be a goose!" Molly teased, giving the middle-aged woman a sound hug. "We love being with you."

"Well, you know my sentiments," Rose admitted. "And I *am* tired. A cold walk holds no appeal this mornin'." She gave Molly a sly look. "Luke seems pretty sweet on you, I'd say."

Molly chose her words carefully. "We're . . . friends."

Rose chuckled. "I may be getting on in years, Molly Wheeler, but I'm not declining into senility. It's plain to me as the nose on your face. Luke Masterson is fallin' in love with you, girl!"

"Now, Rose . . . ," Molly protested, flushing, even as her pulse quickened at the thought.

But the woman was not to be dissuaded. "'Tis only natural," she said. "After all, 'tis easy to love someone who loved you first. Luke's only respondin' to the natural affection you have for him."

"Of course I love him," Molly said with an airy wave of her hand. "Unconditionally, as I would any fellow being God created."

"Molly, Molly," Rose said, shaking her head in mock dismay. "It's much more than that. I can see it even if you and your dear Mr. Masterson cannot. I'm thinkin' it might be nice if you'd invite your beau to dine at the hotel . . . gratis, naturally. After all, you're part of this family, and you don't have any other home for him to come callin' on you. So he's welcome here. And if you don't chance to tell him, I certainly will."

"We'll see," Molly demurred. "I don't intend to be a forward woman, like some of the painted ladies at the Black Diamond. It's up to Luke."

Rose gave an indignant sniff. "Not if I have anything to do with it!"

"You really *are* cut from the same bolt of cloth as Lizzie, the woman from down home I've told you so much about. She was always a great one to turn her hand at matchmaking, given half a chance. 'Course, she claimed it was because she wanted everyone to be as happily married as she was."

"She has her reasons . . . and I have mine," Rose murmured, "and it's a different kettle of fish altogether. I only hope no woman would have to live out the misery I've known, linked with a man not chosen for me by the Lord, but by someone else . . . and for all the wrong reasons. I told you sometime I'd tell you about my past," she promised. "Mayhap I will, soon."

Molly nodded. "We'll have lots of evenings to spend together when Luke is away on his trip."

"Well, we shan't have to worry about my Bert, that's for sure. I declare, but he's spendin' less and less time at home." There was a worried look on Rose's face. "God only knows what he's up to . . . and I'm sure *I'm* happier *not* knowin'."

Luke arrived a moment later, and by the time Molly glanced at the pregnant woman, Rose's perennially happy smile was in place.

Gallantly Luke gave Molly, Rose, and the young Grant girls a hand up into the wagon, causing Rose's youthful daughters to giggle coyly.

"I'll be the envy of the town," he said, chuckling, "attending church in the company of a wagonload of good and beautiful women!"

"Then it's only fitting that a gent such as yourself take a place as guest of honor at Rose Grant's table . . . surrounded by the selfsame beauties!" Rose invited.

Luke cocked his head. "That sounds very much like an invitation to Sunday dinner, ma'am."

"It is! It is!" chorused the girls.

Luke bowed low, sending them into paroxysms of giggles. "Then I accept . . . with pleasure."

"The pleasure is ours!" Rose assured him.

But Molly merely smiled quietly and savored her little secret—that Luke had taken her hand to warm it in his.

No one made any teasing remarks about Luke's appearance at the church service, and for that Molly was grateful. He said little, but seemed to listen with rapt attention to all that was said. He had no Bible of his own and Molly leaned close to share her Good Book with him. She made a mental note to inquire at the mercantile about a Bible for him. Luke needed his own bound volume of the sacred Scriptures, else how would he come to know the Lord?

They lingered after the service, chatting with other worshipers, and Molly was fairly bursting with happiness by the time they returned to the hotel.

Luke insisted that Rose and Molly permit him to help with the clean-up after the noon dining hour. Because they finished quickly, Molly's afternoon break was longer than usual. Instead of retiring to her quarters, she was grateful when Rose suggested that they sit around the fire and talk, or play a game of checkers.

"This fire feels good," Luke said, warming his hands at the hearth.

"And it was plumb chilly in the church building this morning, too," observed Rose.

"Yes, it was," Luke commented, "and I also noticed that the woodpile has dwindled, which has given me an idea for a suitable punishment for the scallywags who made Molly and me the butt of their malicious joke. They're good men and I'd hate for the company to lose them. So I think the best solution all around would be to assign them the task of providing a cord of firewood apiece to the local church, compliments of Sven Larson, Bjorn Olafson, and Ole Anderson."

"A grand idea!" Rose exclaimed, beaming her pleasure.

Molly, too, was complimentary. "It's a fitting punishment. You're a wise and just man, Luke Masterson."

He shrugged aside their praise. "The idea didn't come to me until I was shivering in church this morning."

Molly gave a light laugh. "I told you the Lord would help you find the right solution."

For a moment Luke looked intensely thoughtful. "That you did, didn't you?" he murmured, pausing before going on. "And in addition, because I'll be leaving the end of this week and don't want to have to worry about my wagonload of womenfolk getting to church in safety, an additional part of the restitution calls for the three 'jacks to hitch up a team and transport my best girls to services. And it wouldn't hurt if the heathens were made to stay, too. A little wisdom from the Good Book is what they need to smooth a few rough edges and help mend their sinful proclivities."

Molly could only stare at him in astonishment. "How thoughtful," she said, grateful that he'd found a way to serve justice and to safeguard Rose Grant's health at the same time.

"But it's a task I'll gladly shoulder again upon my return," Luke said.

Mention of his departure made Molly feel suddenly sad. How she was going to miss him! She hoped he would miss her, too, although she wasn't as secure in that knowledge as Rose seemed to be. Why, in the big cities, a man like Luke could have his pick of women, some of whom would make Molly, at her best, look like a wallflower, she thought sadly.

She tried not to let the fearsome thoughts overwhelm her, and as the coming days passed, she focused no further ahead than the immediate evening when she'd be able to enjoy Luke's company in the kitchen and savor a few moments with him in front of the hearth before he went home for the night.

"I'm going to miss our evenings together," Luke confessed the night before he was due to leave on the CNR train mid-morning of the next day.

"And I will miss them, too," Molly sighed. Then, fearing she had appeared too forward, she hastened to explain.

"You–you've been so much help in the kitchen. But I'm going to insist that Rose continue to retire early."

"Be sure Becky helps you."

"I'm sure she will. But if not, I can manage."

They sat, contemplating the crackling fire on the hearth before Luke spoke again, breaking the comfortable silence. "These evenings give me a reason to look forward to returning to Williams, Molly. I know that not long ago, you said you didn't know how long you'd stay in these parts. But please promise me you won't leave while I'm away."

"Of–of course not," Molly stammered. How could he think she'd leave Rose . . . or him? But she felt thrilled that he was looking forward to picking up where he left off upon his return.

"Would you mind terribly if I wrote to you?" Luke inquired.

"Oh, no, I wouldn't mind!" breathed Molly. "I adore getting mail."

"I'm so accustomed to spending time with you evenings, Molly, that it will seem only natural if I pick up pen and paper in my lonely hotel room and share my thoughts with you."

Molly dropped her gaze, glowing in the warmth of his attentions.

"And this way," Luke continued, "you won't have to await my return to learn my progress in finding a physician and a pastor for the town."

"I have a good feeling about your trip, Luke. The Lord will guide you well . . . if only you trust him."

"It's not easy, though, is it?"

Molly smiled softly. "Not always."

"But I'm learning," he said as he arose and crossed to the hall tree.

"I know you are." She rose and followed him.

"I'll miss being with you tomorrow night, Molly, so do you think I could see you in the morning?"

"I'd like that," she whispered, her heart skipping a beat.

"I'll take my breakfast at the hotel. And if you wish and Rose Grant is willing, you could accompany me to the train and see me off."

Molly smiled. "Of course."

"And it will be a consolation in the weeks we're apart, my dear Molly, if I can hope that you'll be waiting at the station when I return, so that your sweet face is the first I see when I come home."

"Lord willing," Molly said fervently, "I'll be there."

chapter

15

Chicago, Illinois

MARC WELLINGHAM SWEPT his blushing bride off her feet and clasped her close, crushing the satiny fabric of her wedding gown. He balanced his precious load carefully, bracing himself against the doorjamb as he twisted the knob, nudged the door open, and carried his new wife across the threshold into the best suite the Drake Hotel had to offer.

Depositing Marissa on her feet, he drew her into his embrace. Then, tilting her face up to his, he leaned over to drop a kiss on the tip of her nose before his lips moved lower to claim her mouth in a lingering kiss that left them both breathless.

"Happy, Mrs. Wellingham?" he inquired as she made murmuring sounds of pleasure.

"Deliriously," she admitted in a breathy whisper. "And you, Dr. Wellingham?"

He gave her a quick squeeze. "I couldn't be happier," he replied, his voice tremulous with emotion.

Marissa searched his face. "You're sure?"

"Positive, my dear! How could you doubt it?"

"Then you're not even a little bit disappointed that ours was not the society wedding of the year?"

Marc laughed. "My darling wife, if anything, I'm *elated*

that it wasn't the social event of the season! Our wedding ceremony was absolutely perfect. Small, but perfect."

Marissa grew wistful at her recollection of the day's events.
"I thought it was lovely, too," she agreed. "But . . . you're
not upset that your mother and Isabelle refused to attend?"

Marc gave an indifferent shrug. "It was their choice. They
were invited, after all."

"I had no kin present, either," Marissa reminded him,
sounding mournful.

She had considered sending her family a telegram, but in
light of the fact that her letter had been ignored, she'd been
unwilling to open herself up to a greater disappointment. So
Marissa's kinfolk, unlike Marc's, had not been invited.

"Silly girl," Marc chided. "We both had family present to
share our joy and witness our holy vows. Our dear brothers
and sisters in Christ wouldn't have missed our nuptials for
anything."

"I'm really going to miss the people from church," Marissa
said. "They're like family to me. And when we move, Marc, I
shan't want to lose touch with them."

"Nor will we," Marc promised. "But wherever we go, we'll
be sure to find good Christian folk."

"I know. And as long as we have each other and our faith,
we'll have everything we need," Marissa sighed, content.

"Forever and for always," Marc promised. "Today is the
happiest day of my life, darling."

"It would be for me, too . . . except . . ." Marissa fell silent.

"Except for what?" Marc prompted.

Marissa's eyes filled with tears. "Except that your family
refused to come to our wedding because you were marrying
me. I was quite acceptable as a servant . . . but completely
*un*acceptable as your wife. Your mother and sister are livid

that you wanted to marry *me* instead of some blue-blooded, silk-stocking, social-register debutante whose fortunes rival your own! Now, because of *me*, your family doesn't approve of *you* any longer. I feel so bad about that, Marc. It's all my fault."

"You're wrong, darling. It's no one's fault. That decision is solely Mother's and Isabelle's. To me, and I hope to you, our love's a blessing. My mother and my stepsister have never really been 'family' to me. There were no bonds of tenderness and no real love to unite us, only tolerance. Since my father's passing, we've been like strangers who simply lived in the same luxurious home."

"And that's another thing!" Marissa moaned. "Adelaide will probably never forgive you for selling the manse."

"Again, Marissa, that was not her decision. I owned the place, for my own mother was a wealthy woman in her own right, and Father preserved the bulk of the estate as my inheritance. As you know, I've found a very suitable home for her in a lovely neighborhood, and Adelaide now owns that house free and clear, plus a handsome financial settlement that should sustain her for the rest of her days . . . if she doesn't dip into the principal too often."

He frowned and strode over to look out the window. "As for the manse, well, I've come to believe that one's possessions sometimes do the possessing." He turned around to look at her, and his expression brightened. "Now that I've disposed of it and Mother and Isabelle are established in their own residence, I feel free. Free to go where the Lord leads, with nothing to tie us down. Free to use my inheritance to purchase the latest medical machines to help suffering people, Marissa. So please don't torment yourself, my dear, for I'm excited. *Excited!*"

Marissa managed a wan smile. "I know you've been exploring possible places to set up your new practice. Have you settled on a town yet?"

"I should know within the next few days."

Marissa could not contain a shuddering sigh of relief. "It will be marvelous to go somewhere where no one knows me, where I'll be accepted for myself and who I am now . . . not judged on who . . . or what . . . I've been in the past."

Marc covered the distance between them in a single stride and swept her into his embrace once again, cradling her head beneath his chin. "Poor darling. With all the wedding plans and my hospital routine, we haven't had much time to talk lately, have we? But the next forty-eight hours belong only to us," he whispered.

He straightened his shoulders and set her at arm's length so he could look into her face. "After that, I'll be meeting with a Mr. Masterson from northern Minnesota. I expect to like him when we finally meet face-to-face, after corresponding for months. Seems to be an honest, forthright fellow. I can tell he's really sold on this region that has become home to him, Marissa," Marc said, his words rushing out in his growing excitement. "He believes that it's an undeveloped area of great potential, although from his descriptions of it, it sounds more like the end of the earth!" A grin split his face. "Perhaps that's why that untamed wilderness, populated by Indians and immigrants from European countries, along with homesteaders, trappers, and lumberjacks appeals to me."

"Is it very far away?"

"A long way from civilization as we know it, I'm afraid," Marc admitted. "The northernmost border area of Minnesota, actually, not far from a great body of water, Lake of the Woods, shared with Canada.

"I'll be honest, darling," he said, his eyes shining, "I'd really like to have a part in developing this land . . . I feel the Lord leading me . . . us . . . to this fledgling town, Williams . . ." Marc paused, frowning. "But we'll not go, Marissa, if you can't share my enthusiasm. For I could never be content knowing my wife was unhappy."

Marissa put her arms around her new husband and pillowed her head on his chest. "Haven't I told you, Marc darling, that where you go, there shall I go? All I need to be happy is you . . . and the opportunity to serve the Lord at your side."

"Well, we seem to be of one mind," Marc whispered, drawing her closer still. "And I long for the day when our children will grow up alongside this brash and bold frontier town."

Williams, Minnesota

The winter wind was howling around the corner of the Grant Hotel when Molly closed the dining room and kitchen for the night. With the blizzard raging outside, the number of diners had dwindled to a very few.

Rose had insisted on staying to help with the chores, and Molly had relented only when the exhausted woman promised to seat herself on a stool so she could dry dishes and set them on a nearby sideboard to be put away later.

One of Rose's sons had gone to the woodshed to fill the woodbox and had then stacked some logs beside the hearth in the lobby to bank the fire through the night. The cheery blaze would keep the hotel warm against the frigid gale that rattled the windows and hurled sleet against the panes of glass.

With their chores behind them, Molly and Rose huddled

close to the fireplace, talking softly as they did handiwork to pass the time.

"I miss that rascal Luke," Rose said, looking up from her knitting to rest her eyes. "And if *I* miss the man, I can only guess how *you* must be pinin' for the sight of him."

Molly sighed deeply. "Each day seems a little longer than the one before."

"And a little gloomier?"

"Y–yes . . . how did you know?"

"You needn't look so surprised, Molly-girl. After all, I was in love once upon a time . . . even if it was long, long ago."

"I'd gathered as much from some remarks you've made," Molly said, hoping to prompt the older woman to share her story.

"I've been meanin' to tell you, but somehow the time never felt quite right," Rose murmured. She sighed and laid her needlework in her lap. "Mayhap now's as good a time as any. If you're wantin' to pass a cold winter's night listenin' to an old lady talk, then roll another log on the fire, dear, and nestle down with your needlepoint while I commence to ramble."

Molly hefted a pine log onto the bed of red-hot coals, then reseated herself. "You're wrong about one thing . . . you're not *old*."

Rose shrugged. "Maybe not . . . but I haven't felt young—or young at heart—in many a year. Not since I turned my back on Homer Ames's offer . . . and, instead, did exactly as my ne'er-do-well, drunken pa ordered, and struck a bargain to become a mail-order bride."

"His name was Homer?" Molly asked softly, after a long pause.

"Yes, and a finer Christian gentleman you'd never hope to meet. Alas, he was rich in faith, but Homer's family was as poor as ours and for the self-same reasons, though his mother tried hard enough, God rest her soul. He came from a family like my own—the mother, a fine Christian woman, and the father, a drunkard who wasted his money on loose women while his family did without." Molly could read the pain in the woman's eyes. "Just like my Bert's no doubt doing this very evening . . . breakin' his marriage pact with me by dallyin' with the painted beauties at the Black Diamond Saloon."

"Homer loved you, too?" Molly asked breathlessly, drawing her back to a happier time.

"Oh, my, yes!" Rose recalled, her eyes growing soft with the memories. "Enough so's he wanted to marry me . . . and *begged* me not to wed a man I didn't even know. But I was young, Molly, and scared. . . ." She turned a stricken look on Molly, "And my pa had made a deal to marry me off. I didn't dare defy him. He'd have taken his razor strop to me and plumb wore it out before he was through with me."

Molly gasped at the naked look of horror. "Oh, Rose . . . how awful for you."

"I was barely past fifteen." Rose's soft voice was husky with unshed tears, contained, Molly sensed, for over half a lifetime. "I told my father I didn't know this Bert fellow the marriage broker mentioned. Told him I loved Homer . . . and Homer loved me." Rose winced. "That's when Pa backhanded me across the face. 'Love!' he said. 'What do you know about love? I can tell you it's as easy to love a rich man as a poor man, and it makes a heap more sense. I'm through providin' for you. It's time *you* provided for *me* by marryin' well'. . ." Her voice trailed off to a harsh whisper. "And then Pa called me . . . a *terrible* name."

Molly was shocked. "Rose . . . you poor dear. You were only a child."

"That I was, but with the body of a young woman. And with a head and heart full of romantic dreams. Growin' up in poverty as we had, the idea of having plenty to eat and wear turned my head, I fear, for I believed I could be content if I had what other folks took for granted. Not only that . . . I was too young and cowed by my bullyin' father, and my mother was too timid to speak up and tell him that the only thing of lastin' value would be the love of a good Christian man."

Rose sighed and shifted her great bulk in the chair. "Besides, I was romantic enough to believe that I'd learn to love Bert like I did Homer. Little did I know that I was throwin' away my only chance for true happiness . . . and would have to suffer for my choice."

"I hadn't thought of that," Molly mused. "I was grown when I decided to become a mail-order bride, without realizing that the freedom to choose is a real privilege . . . a special gift of grace."

"Homer was tore up when I told him what I had to do," Rose went on. "His eyes filled with tears . . . and him a grown man, four years older than me. He looked plumb heartsick . . . as wretched as I felt myself. Then he was crushin' me to him, kissin' me like he'd never dared before and tellin' me how much he loved me. Begged me to run away with him, too. Admitted he was only a poor boy but vowed to work hard and make somethin' of himself . . . for my sake. Homer told me that with his faith in God and with me by his side, he could do anything. . . ." She choked at the memory, then straightened her shoulders. "Well, you can guess the rest. I did the easy thing . . . out of fear of my pa's wrath . . . and ended up hitched to Bert Grant. Spent my weddin' night alone—which was all right with me—for Pa and Bert went to the saloon to celebrate, with Bert spendin' his greenbacks on loose women and strong drink."

Rose turned from contemplating the fire to gaze at Molly with a troubled expression on her face. "You know, I wondered why Bert had ordered himself a mail-order bride, when he wasn't a bad-lookin' sort in his prime. And he was free enough with his funds to capture many a saloon gal. But I figured it out soon enough." Her face set, she continued, "He invested most of his inheritance in this hotel. Crafty man that he is, he just plain married to get a good and honest woman to work hard in his business, support him, and keep a decent home—for when he felt like returnin' to it—someone who'd be thrifty with the family finances so's there'd be plenty of jack for him to idle away his nights at his pleasures."

"Oh, Rose . . . I don't know what to say," murmured Molly. "How have you been able to stand it all these years?"

Rose blinked back tears and swallowed hard. "It's been a rugged cross to bear, Molly. But I gave my vow to stand by Bert from that day forward, in sickness and in health, and for better or worse. Yessir, Molly, I accepted the man for better or for worse. But child that I was, I had no notion how much worse it would be! And of course, my mama didn't tell me. Didn't dare, I guess, for she'd have had Pa to deal with."

Silence fell between them as the women worked on, their fingers flying, keeping time to their roiling thoughts.

"Whatever became of Homer?" Molly blurted out at last. "Did he marry and find happiness?"

"Homer did just as he'd predicted that day when he begged me to elope with him. He worked hard, was true to his faith, kept his honor, and now he's an officer in one of the biggest banks in Fargo, North Dakota. But he did it all alone . . . without a wife at his side." Rose sighed. "He's had a good life . . . knowin' that comforts my broken heart . . . but he's never married and that causes me pain. For I feel that, lovin' me as he did and bein' denied, I robbed him of a home and family."

"Very probably he still loves you," Molly said thoughtfully.

"Loves the memory of the girl he knew, not the woman I am now," Rose said bitterly, but with a trace of wistfulness.

"And a part of you still loves him?"

The older woman turned an anguished look on Molly. "Right or wrong, Molly-girl, I can't help myself. But we don't see each other, although we exchange Christmas cards every Yuletide season . . . me lettin' Homer think I'm a lot happier than I actually am."

"It must be hard . . . loving someone, but not being free to know true happiness together."

"That's why I generally spend my days tryin' hard *not* to remember," Rose snorted.

"Once you really love someone like that," Molly said reflectively, "I reckon you can't just stop, simply because circumstances have changed. You can't keep your heart from aching with loss simply because it isn't correct or convenient."

"Exactly," Rose sadly agreed. "Homer and I haven't been able to link up in this life, since I foolishly found myself unequally yoked with an unbeliever. But I can't help prayin' that we'll both remain staunch in our faith so the day will come when we'll be together again . . . if not 'til we're gathered in glory 'round the Great White Throne."

"What a lovely thought."

"And I draw comfort from knowin' that the Lord can bring great good out of bad choices. Even when we've gone against his ways, we may find that it paved the way for a miracle so's we can praise his name." Rose's eyes shone. "I didn't plan all my young'uns," she admitted, "but I've welcomed each and every one, for I knew that our Creator had a special purpose for 'em from the time they were given life in my womb."

They sat again in silence, basking in the warmth of the fire and of Rose's sage words. Gradually the topic turned away from the past and the women talked of more trivial things, neither wanting to disrupt the intimacy of the moment with thoughts of bedtime.

Finally, when the grandfather clock gonged the midnight hour, Rose boosted her ample girth from her chair. "Well, it appears that husband of mine isn't comin' home again tonight. The Lord will have to watch over him, for I'm unable now. Used to be, Molly, I'd throw on a wrap and hie myself on over to the saloon, rain or shine, fightin' everything from heat and mosquitoes to a winter blizzard. I'd pluck him out of that den of iniquity and bring him safely home to sleep off his transgressions. But I can't risk the welfare of the comin' babe to protect a husband who'd only resent me for carin'. Even so . . . I can't help worryin' about him . . . at least a little."

Molly considered Rose's plight and for a split second she was about to offer to brave the fearsome blizzard and make her way to the saloon to fetch Bert Grant back herself. But a moment later she realized that it would be a futile and foolish undertaking. As heavily as the snow was falling now, the glow of a lantern would be swallowed up, and she could easily become lost in the dark and perish.

Obviously Rose Grant had consigned her husband's fate to the Lord and Molly knew she must, too. She could do nothing tonight except pray that Rose would be strengthened in

her trials and that Bert Grant would somehow see the light
. . . before it was too late.

chapter

16

THE BLIZZARD RAGED for two full days and part of a third before the sun finally appeared, leaving the pine-studded landscape draped beneath a heavy snowfall. Drifts mounded in the street, and ice crusted over snow that had been driven into the sleet, then frozen to an opaque glaze on steamy streets and windowpanes.

On the morning of the third day, the residents exited their cabins, houses, and business establishments and began to shovel out.

"Bert will probably be home now," Rose observed, "if for no other reason than to collect some cash from the safe so's he can go back to the saloon."

Molly couldn't bring herself to respond to the bleak comment. She'd noticed the dark circles that had appeared under her friend's eyes and knew that while Rose had retired to her room each night, she had had little rest.

"Perhaps the train will make it through today," Molly said, attempting to distract Rose's somber thoughts, "and the mail will come in."

"That would be a treat." Rose brightened. "Likely you'll hear from Luke."

"Or from Lizzie or Mary Katharine."

"We get little mail ourselves," Rose admitted, "though sometimes our patrons get letters sent in care of General Delivery. So when you check with the postmaster, would you be so kind as to bring ours along? It'll spare me bravin' the elements to attend to it myself."

A few hours later, Molly heard the bellow of the approaching train as it proceeded from Cedar Spur toward Williams, a few miles farther to the east. The train's wail sounded thin as the noise was carried on the frigid air.

Molly put on overshoes, snugged her heavy coat about her, drew a woolen cap over her wavy hair, and gratefully accepted a scarf from Rose. Outside, the temperature was below zero, and she dropped her chin against the icy breeze that felt several degrees lower.

It was quite a little walk to the post office where she would await the sorting of the incoming mail scheduled to arrive on the Canadian National Train. Molly carefully picked her way down the steps, cleared by Rose's eldest boy. She stepped through the high drifts, powdery snow clinging to her cotton stockings and causing them to dampen beneath the long skirts that trailed in the snow.

By the time she neared the mercantile, Molly was gasping, her breaths becoming white plumes in the frosty air. The thought of the roaring pot-bellied stove hurried her steps, and she was looking forward to the warm blaze that would help thaw her as she waited for the postmaster to finish his sorting duties.

Nearing the depot, Molly heard a shrill cry go up from the knot of people awaiting the incoming train as it chugged to a stop, fanning a spray of snow into the air. She glanced toward the crowd, then back toward the locomotive as it nosed ahead, plowing through the drifts that had mounded over the tracks in spots.

What Molly thought had been a sound of exultation was,

she discovered a moment later, an outcry of horror. For she whirled in time to see a body topple from the train's steel cow-catcher, the corpse unceremoniously deposited on the railbed, like a stiff rag doll flung there by a toy train. Except that this was no doll!

"It's Bert!" she heard a lumberjack shout. "Bert Grant! He's dead as a mackerel! Froze stiff as a block of ice, he is! Well, now we don't have to wonder where he's been keepin' hisself the past two days. The last drink he had to warm him for the walk home didn't keep him from freezin' to death, poor sod. The bonny girls at the saloon will sore miss him and his free-spendin' ways."

"Oh, no!" Molly gasped, feeling as if she'd just been kicked by a Missouri mule. And she stood, stunned, in the middle of the street, unsure of what to do, where to go.

How could Rose bear this unexpected tragedy? And who would tell her of her husband's fate?

As Molly stood rooted in confusion, she looked around for assistance. And when she glanced again at the grisly scene, Bert's corpse was gone.

Seeing a motley group of lumberjacks shouldering a burden and realizing that they were hauling Rose's late husband's remains to the Grant Hotel, Molly cried out in protest. "No! Wait! Please don't! You can't just march in there and . . ." But as she turned into the northerly wind, the sound of her plea failed to reach the woodsmen who were fast approaching the stoop leading into the town's only hotel.

Molly tried to run but her weak leg gave out, and she toppled into a snowdrift, plunging her arms into the fresh-fallen snow up to her shoulders. Her face, colliding with a sharp crust of ice, burned, and she wrestled to extricate herself. Hot tears scalded her cheeks and began to freeze on her lashes.

Over and over again, Molly slipped and slid as she struggled through the snow, crying out with the painful wrenching of her weakened leg, feeling as if she were trapped in a nightmare from which there was no awakening.

She knew she was too late when a keening wail emanated through the open doors leading into the lobby of the hotel. No doubt the lumberjacks, probably in their cups to the point where they didn't consider a pregnant woman's sensibilities, had dropped the frozen Bert on the Olson rug in the parlor, like a stick of stovewood.

Molly, gasping for breath as she rushed up the steps, was almost knocked down by the men on their way out of the hotel. Shaken, she entered to see Rose collapsed on the floor, crying hysterically, her tears falling onto Bert's ghastly pale face.

"He's dead!" Rose wailed. "Oh, dear Lord, he's *dead*! What'll I do . . . ? Oh, Molly, what'll I do?"

The next hour was a nightmare for everyone in the hotel. Molly knew she would be eternally grateful to Mr. Lundsten, the owner of the mercantile, who came by upon hearing of the tragedy and quickly took charge, ordering passersby to help him fetch a pine box from the storage area behind the store. Then, gently disengaging Rose's hands from her husband's shirt, they lowered Bert's remains into the box.

Lumberjacks from the Black Diamond, Bert's cronies, volunteered to use picks and grubbing hoes to wrest a grave from the frozen ground so his body might be interred in the cemetery on the edge of town.

Quietly Mr. Lundsten suggested that Molly help Rose to her private quarters. And, like a child, the woman allowed herself to be led away.

"Give her some laudanum or some Lydia Pinkham's tonic," advised the merchant. "And if I've anything in the store to assist you, 'tis yours for the takin'. I just wish we had a doc in town to attend Mrs. Grant."

"No more than I," agreed Molly. "She looks to be in a bad way."

Mr. Lundsten nodded. "Nigh on as bad as Bert . . . and him dead . . . though I shouldn't wonder that she won't join him before long."

Molly saw him to the door, her mind swirling like the snowflakes captured by the blizzard-force winds and carried about against their will. As she hurried down the hall to Rose's suite, she stilled her thoughts by whispering the Psalms to herself.

Rose had swooned onto the bed and eventually fell into a restless sleep from which she awakened occasionally in panicky alarm, only to lapse again into unconsciousness. Molly scarcely left her side, asking Becky to post a notice that no meals would be served at the Grant Hotel that evening.

The stars were glimmering bright in the inky night sky when a knock sounded at the front door. Molly had just left Becky to care for her mother while Molly went around and banked the various woodstoves and fireplaces. Crossing to the door, she peered out. It was Mr. Lundsten, who had been such a godsend that afternoon.

"Thought I'd stop by to see how Mrs. Grant is doing," he explained when she swung the door open and he stepped inside, stomping the snow off his boots. "We're sorry about the mister. He was no pillar of society, but he was created by God, same's anyone else, and it's a pity for any soul to perish like that."

"A true tragedy."

"I thank the good Lord she's got you, Miss Molly, for I don't rightly know how she'd endure otherwise."

"I'm not sure she will," Molly said, acknowledging her fear for the first time. "I'm terrified for Rose. She takes on awfully when she has a lucid moment, though she seems to be in another world most of the time—and that's likely for the best—so she's not having to dwell on what happened this afternoon. But she's not a well woman."

The merchant nodded in solemn agreement. "I hope Mr. Masterson has some luck finding a physician for our town. We could use his services now."

"I'm praying daily that he will," Molly said, "just as I'm praying that the Lord will help Rose hold on. Her children need her."

"And that may just give her the will to live." Mr. Lundsten shifted from one foot to the other, and Molly noticed the postal bag strapped on his back. "I wanted to inquire about Mrs. Grant, of course," he went on, "but I also stopped to leave off some mail that came for you, Miss Molly." He produced a packet of letters from an inner pocket of his greatcoat.

"How thoughtful of you. I was on my way to see about the mail when I saw . . . Bert's . . ." Molly shuddered in revulsion and her voice trailed away.

"I thought that's how it was," Mr. Lundsten said kindly. "So I figured this was the least I could do. A body feels rather helpless in times like this."

"There's little anyone can do except pray and let Rose know we're standing by." Molly thanked the man and closed the door securely behind him.

Taking the letters with her, Molly returned to Rose's room to relieve Becky. Rose didn't move when Molly called her name, but lay in bed as one dead.

Seating herself in the rocking chair drawn up to the bed,

Molly drew the coal oil lamp nearer, then sheafed through the letters. There was one from Katie, another from Lizzie, and a third from Luke! Scanning the first two hurriedly, she saved Luke's letter, posted from St. Paul, for last.

"My darling Molly," he wrote,

> I am in good health, and I hope this missive finds you the same. My trip to St. Paul was uneventful and the weather pleasant for this time of year. My schedule has been busy, and this is the first evening when I have had a chance to take pen in hand to contact, although you are never far from my thoughts.
>
> I have met with Pastor Theodore Edgerton, and you will be heartened to know that he has accepted the call to serve the small congregation in Williams. It was not a hard bargain negotiated. I simply told Ted—an old friend from the past—of our dire need for a man of God, and after giving the matter prayerful thought, he gave me his decision the next day. He and his wife, Emily, will be arriving in Williams not long after my return, praise God!
>
> Ted's the closest thing to a brother I have, since we grew up together in the Orphan's Home. But as we both agree, while we may not be blood kin, something has happened that makes me know we're closer kin than that! While I've been away from you, dear Molly, I've had much time to consider my eternal destiny and have come to the conclusion that I must put things right with the Lord. This I have done, poring over the little Bible you pressed in my hand just before I left. Now, I know that you and Ted and I are all brothers and sisters in Christ. . . .

Molly put the letter down, unable to see for the sudden sheen of glad tears misting her eyes. When she cleared her vision, she read on eagerly.

> Now if I can just arrange for a physician with the same ease, I'll know for a certainty that the Lord is guiding my steps, just as you predicted he would. I trust that such a man may have already received a "call" and is just waiting for a human contact. It is my

goal to have a physician practicing in Williams before our dear friend, Rose Grant, gives birth. She'll feel more confident with a medical school graduate attending her needs, for Mrs. Woolery has confided in me that she is a little worried about complications.

I shall write you in another day or two and hope that mail service is such that I won't arrive home before this communique!

Give the townspeople my greetings and feel free to share the good news about the new pastor. Give Rose my warmest regards and know that you, Molly, are the object of my utmost respect, affectionate thoughts, and now my gratitude as well.—Luke

Molly read and reread the letter through the long hours of the night, quietly thanking the Lord for Luke's salvation. She wasn't sure when she fell asleep, but the grayness of dawn had invaded the dim room when she awoke. The coal oil lamp was burning low, the flame flickering on the wick.

Molly winced as she eased herself into a more comfortable position, testing her stiff joints. She tried to rise to see about Rose, but her leg was cramped and numb. For a moment she thought the groan she heard was her own as her limb suddenly throbbed to life with stinging, prickling sensations. Then she realized that the deathly moan had emanated from Rose Grant.

Her own pains forgotten, Molly sprang up and limped to the bed. Rose's complexion was as pale as clabbered milk. "Oh, no!" Molly whispered, her pulses hammering at her temples. She would have believed Rose dead, except that the woman gave another moan, proof that there was still life in her body, though not for long.

Steeling herself, Molly threw back the covers. In spite of all she could do, she could not stifle the scream that rose within, for there was blood. *So much blood!*

Becky came running in, garbed only in her flannel night-dress, her tangled hair flying about her sleep-encrusted eyes.

"Quick! Raise one of your brothers!" Molly cried. "Send him for help! Maybe Mrs. Woolery will know what to do!"

"Is—is it bad?" Becky stammered, her lower lip trembling.

"It's a matter of life and death," Molly sobbed. "The baby's lost . . . but we mustn't lose your mama, too!"

Becky quickly returned with her brother Samuel, who raced in, took one look, and tore away, ashen-faced with fright.

"Is there anything I can do?" Becky whimpered, wringing her hands.

"Pray, honey, like you've never prayed before," Molly said. "Pray for a miracle . . . for your mama needs one now." And under her breath, she added, "With all she's been through, Rose Grant deserves to know a little earthly happiness before she goes on to Paradise."

In the following days that quickly became one week, then two, Mrs. Woolery and Molly took turns nursing Rose. Between the two of them, and with the help of the Grant daughters and even the sons, who seemed suddenly sober and more supportive of their mother than ever before, the hotel remained open.

"I think she's going to make it, even though the babe did not," said Sonya Woolery on the fifteenth day of Rose's confinement. "But she won't have an easy time of it. As far as her health has declined, she'll be a long time bouncing back from this ordeal."

Molly nodded wearily. Rose had had no appetite, and they'd managed only to spoon small amounts of broth and gruel into her for sustenance. Her once-plump cheeks now seemed sunken, and her former rosy coloring was now pale as parchment. But at least she was alive. And the tired women who tended her drew some comfort from that fact, praying that the situation would not be further complicated by sepsis.

"It looks likely we'll have a physician soon," Molly said, quoting from her most recent letter from Luke, who was due to return to Williams in another week or two, right before the Christmas holidays.

"Well, it can't be too soon for me," Sonya sighed. "I'd gladly turn this case over to one more qualified, for I feel woefully inadequate."

"You can't blame yourself," Molly protested. "You've done a good job."

"Not I . . . the Lord deserves the credit, for I feared for her life more than once."

The days were so full with work, worry, and the exhausting task of attending to Rose's needs that Molly had little time for herself or for fussing over holiday treats or decorations. Her nightly diary entries were sketchy but diligently recorded, and Luke's letters arrived with heart-warming regularity, proving a lifeline to her. She pined for his return in a way she'd never longed for another. Luke Masterson made her feel whole, and without him, she was less than complete.

Each day, if there were no new missives to add to the batch Molly kept in an ornate gilt box beside her bed, she reread her old ones from Luke and her family. And each day she collected the Grants' mail, along with her own, and dutifully read Rose's cards and letters to the weakened woman.

But Molly made sure Rose was alone when she found one addressed to the Grant family—a Christmas card and letter from Mr. Homer Ames of Fargo, North Dakota! It was a lavishly embellished card, elegant and expensive, a gauge of the wealth of the man who had sent it.

"You have a card from Homer," Molly reported, seating herself on the edge of Rose's bed.

"Oh . . . Homer. I haven't even *thought* of Christmas cards," Rose moaned dully. "I don't know if I can manage the strength to write to him. And if he doesn't hear from me, he'll worry that something's wrong."

"I–I could write to him on your behalf," Molly offered, "until, of course, you're able to pen a note for yourself."

Rose looked at her through eyes that suddenly filled with tears of gratitude. "Would you? You'll know what to say, Molly."

"It's the least I can do for you," Molly said and patted the woman's now-skinny shoulder. "You concern yourself only with getting well. Luke will be home soon, and you want to be healthy enough to smile for him, don't you?"

"Yes," Rose murmured, "though we all know, Molly-girl . . . that he only has eyes for you."

Later that night, when Molly retired to her room, she ruined three sheets of stationery in trying to write Homer Ames, aborting the attempt almost as soon as she'd begun setting pen to paper.

"Dear God," she whispered miserably, "please help me find the right words."

Then, recalling the story Rose had told her, Molly dwelt on the fact that she and Homer were both believers, united in their faith in the Lord and their shared love for Rose, and with a sudden sense of confidence, she began.

Molly introduced herself to Rose's old friend by explaining that she had only recently come into Rose's life as a new friend. After that, the words seemed to flow miraculously.

Though she did not mention it in her letter, she entertained a secret fond hope for Rose and Homer, but relinquished their future to the Lord as she signed and sealed the envelope. Their lives would come together or drift apart in accordance with his plans and the web and weft of human choices.

Molly made plans to post the letter early, arriving in time to meet the incoming Canadian National Railroad train in case Luke should be on it.

For four days now, she had been disappointed. But one sweet day soon, Luke Masterson would light from the coach, and she would be there to welcome him back to her world.

chapter
17

As Christmas Eve day drew near, Molly felt increasingly anxious at the thought that Luke might not return in time to celebrate the Savior's birth with the congregation that comprised the little church of Williams.

As she went about her work, Molly listened for the wail of the arriving train. She had not heard its approach and was unaware of its arrival until she heard it chug away from the depot and continue west toward Warroad.

Molly ran to the window, and her disappointment grew even more keen when she didn't see Luke Masterson among the knot of people still standing on the siding.

Resolutely she went about her business, basting the turkey and preparing the stuffing that she would be serving later that day. Even though Rose was still not able to do the cooking, Molly was determined that hotel guests and other patrons of the dining room would be able to enjoy a traditional holiday meal, even if far from family and friends, just as she was this blessed season.

So preoccupied was she with her task that she was caught unaware when the door opened and soft footsteps approached. She turned to greet the newcomer—Luke!

Her lips parted in surprise. "Oh, Luke, I'm sorry! I fully intended to meet you at the station, but I didn't know the train had arrived. I didn't hear the whistle."

"I asked the engineer not to blow it. You see, I changed my mind about having you meet me."

Molly's heart sank. Maybe he had met someone else while he was away, she thought. Someone much prettier and slimmer. . . . She couldn't help feeling hurt but was really perplexed when his eyes lit with irrepressible good humor.

Ignoring his peculiar behavior, Molly quickly sketched in what had transpired since he'd left Williams—Bert's grisly death, Rose's declining health.

"Then in light of the grim news, Molly, I'm especially glad that I have some wonderful surprises for you."

"Surprise? For me?" she asked, frowning in confusion.

"Who else?" he teased.

"What did you bring me?"

"Something from Chicago, my sweet. Actually," he said, and his grin widened, "two things from Chicago. No, make it *three*."

Relieved that Luke was his old self, Molly felt like a child anticipating Christmas morning. She thought of the gift she'd made for Luke and the inexpensive but handy items purchased at the mercantile. She would present these to him as a remembrance of this first special Christmas together.

"You'll have your surprises very shortly," Luke promised. "The first, momentarily; the second, after we have a wonderful dinner at our usual table in the hotel, and the third, when we go to church for the Christmas Eve service."

Almost as if on cue, the front door opened. "Well, well," Luke said, "come in, Dr. Wellingham. Your patient awaits you in her quarters."

"The physician?" Molly gasped.

"Yes. Since the good doctor had nothing to detain him in Chicago, he decided to accompany me to Williams. I wanted to save him for a surprise. That's why we hoped to slip into town without your being any the wiser."

Molly laughed with delight. "Then I forgive your deceit," she said, leading the way to Rose's suite and making the introductions, before leaving the physician to examine the sick woman in privacy.

When Dr. Wellingham returned to the lobby where Molly and Luke were catching up on what had taken place during their long separation, Molly got to her feet and hurried to bring another cup of coffee and a plate of Christmas delicacies.

"Molly, Dr. Marcus Wellingham, formerly of Chicago, is one of Williams's newest residents and among the most welcome, I might add. Marc, this beautiful lady originally hails from your Prairie State."

"It's a pleasant surprise to meet a former resident of my home state," Dr. Wellingham said pleasantly. "Where in Illinois did you live?"

"Downstate in Effingham County," Molly replied. "I lived in Watson, a small town, and in Effingham, also, the county seat, before I came to these parts."

"Ah, I've heard of both those towns, although I've never traveled there myself."

"Now that we've enjoyed our surprise," Luke said, "I imagine you'd like to officially register at the Grant Hotel, Marc, right?"

"Very much so!"

Molly arose and led the way into the hotel lobby. "We can attend to that right away."

"My wife and I would like the nicest suite available," said Dr. Wellingham. "And we'll be needing it for an extended period, since I'm not sure how long it'll be until we're able to find a permanent home in which to set up a practice."

"You're welcome here for as long as you care to stay, Dr. Wellingham, and I'm looking forward to making your wife's acquaintance, too. I hope she'll be as happy in Williams as I am."

The doctor cocked an appraising eye. "I have a feeling that you and Mrs. Wellingham will be the best of friends, like sisters, actually, for I'd say that the two of you have a great deal in common. My wife is a most agreeable woman, if I do say so myself."

"Having met both lovely women," Luke chimed in, "I believe I can almost guarantee it, Marc. What do you say we return to my place and haul your trunks to the hotel so you can get settled while Mrs. Wellingham stays at my house to rest up from her long trip?"

"I do hope your wife is not ill," Molly said with concern.

"A bit tired from the trip is the extent of it," Dr. Wellingham assured her. "Luke was telling us about the Christmas candlelight ceremony at the church this evening, and Mrs. Wellingham wanted to be rested sufficiently to attend."

"I'll be looking forward to making her acquaintance then."

After the two men left, Molly savored the surprise of the physician's arrival, earlier than anticipated, and couldn't help wondering what other surprises Luke had in store. Her thoughts swirled with possibilities and her labors seemed light as she flew through her chores, stopping only when Marc and Luke reappeared to lug the big trunk to the Wellingham suite.

When Luke returned shortly before closing time, Molly served him his meal, joining him, then lingering over coffee as he told her about his trip.

After she cleared away the plates and returned to the table,

208

she found a small, gift-wrapped box at her place. "For you, Molly," Luke murmured. "Surprise number two."

With trembling fingers, she opened the tiny package. Inside, nestled on a bed of deep blue velvet, a brilliant diamond set in yellow gold winked up at her as bright and clear as a star in the winter sky.

"It's an engagement ring, darling. I purchased it in the fervent hope that you would agree to become my wife. The diamond is a precious stone, Molly, but it pales beside your worth in my life."

"Oh, Luke!" Molly looked across the table at him, her eyes shimmering with happy tears. Then unable to restrain herself, she abandoned her chair and threw herself into his waiting, welcoming arms.

Minutes flew by like seconds as Molly remained in Luke's embrace, and they laughed and whispered, happily planning their future together.

"We're going to have to part now, Molly dear," Luke said, "although I eagerly anticipate the time when we'll never be separated again. I must get ready for the service tonight, then I'll return to fetch you and any of Rose's children who want to attend this evening."

"It will be a cutter full," Molly warned, "for 'tis not just the girls and I who are planning to go, but Rose's sons, too."

"Their father's death had a major effect on them, didn't it?"

Molly nodded. "I believe it caused them to give a thought to their own young lives . . . and conclude that they didn't wish to die as their pa had."

"Well, Molly, I'll be around to guide them however I'm able," Luke promised.

She smiled fondly at him. "I knew you'd feel that way. And Mr. Lundsten said as much."

"No doubt Marc will lend a hand, as well. And soon we'll have a pastor to help shepherd the young ones."

Molly's heart skipped a beat moments after Luke had left the Grant Hotel to go to his own cozy dwelling on the edge of town. Could that be the third surprise he had promised? Could it possibly be that Pastor Edgerton, too, had made arrangements to arrive in time to service his little flock on the eve of their Savior's birth?

With that thought in the forefront of her mind, Molly dressed hastily and mother-henned the progress of the Grant children until they were all polished within an inch of their lives, ready to depart as soon as Luke arrived.

"All aboard!" he called out merrily after he assisted Molly and the Grant girls into the cutter and Rose's sons scrambled in behind.

Then he snapped the reins smartly against the mare's back, and she moved down the street at a brisk pace.

At the church, Luke helped Molly and the girls from the cutter while the boys hopped down and joined the other worshipers moving slowly into the small building.

"Save me a space on the pew," Luke said. "I'll return momentarily. I promised to give a few others a ride to services."

Puzzled, Molly watched him leave, begrudging every moment they were apart after such a long absence. And the congregation was about to lift their voices in the opening hymn before Molly heard the church door open, and a rush of icy wind announced the arrival of the latecomers.

Luke slipped into the pew beside Molly and opened the hymnal. She heard some shifting and hitching as the late-arriving worshipers took their seats in the back and the services began. Gradually the church building grew warm, not only from the fire in the woodstove, but from the fervor of the congregation, joined in love and faith on this most blessed of all nights.

When the new pastor did not make a grand entrance to conduct the service, Molly realized that Pastor Edgerton's arrival was not Luke's third surprise, after all. And just before she focused on the reading of the Christmas story from the sacred Scriptures, she wondered again what it might be.

When the service concluded and the celebrants were exchanging cheerful Yuletide greetings, Molly spotted Dr. Wellingham and his wife at a distance, surrounded by a crowd of parishioners who were making the new physician's acquaintance. The couple would have been obscured from view, had it not been for Marc Wellingham's great height.

"Let's go see the good doctor and his wife," Luke whispered. "I've invited them to accompany us back to the hotel. Maybe we could have something warm to thaw us after the cold drive."

Molly smiled up at him. "What fun! I've been wanting to meet Mrs. Wellingham, and this will give us a chance to get to know each other."

As they approached, some of the town's residents bade the doctor and his wife good-bye and stepped out into the clear, wintry night.

Turning her gaze in the direction of the couple, Molly felt her heart flutter and, for a breathless moment, she felt as if her bad leg would give way beneath her. Mrs. Marc Wellingham bore a striking resemblance to her sister Marissa! She had the same burnished curls feathering about her face, the same sparkling eyes, the same quick lift of her head as she laughed up into her husband's face. What trick of the candle-light, still glowing in the windows, had conspired to make Molly believe that this woman could be her long-lost twin?

But as she took a few steps nearer, she knew for a certainty. It *was* Marissa! Oh, miracle of miracles, Marc Wellingham had taken as his bride Marissa Wheeler, her own sister!

Beside herself with joy, Molly rushed toward the poised young woman, crying out her name, "Marissa! Marissa!"

Only when the young doctor's wife stiffened did Molly realize that she had not been recognized. "Do I know you?" Marissa inquired, her brow arched in confusion.

Molly would have been crushed except that, in the next instant, the truth dawned. Marissa did not know her sister because Molly's appearance had changed so drastically since their last meeting. And not only was she slimmer and more svelte than ever before, but she was stylishly dressed and more confident than the little girl who had lived on the banks of Salt Creek.

"Heavens, Marissa!" Molly cried, laughing. "I hope you're not getting as daft as Miss Abby in her later years. For if you are, we'll certainly have our hands full . . . as full as Pa and Miss Lizzie and Brad have with their brood. And my Luke will have to make sure he never loans you any horses belonging to the lumber company, for he'd risk you selling them for a song just as sure as I'm Molly Wheeler!"

As the familiar names and references came swirling out of the past, a kaleidoscope of emotions played across Marissa's face, and she looked into the sweet face, saw the well-remembered features so like her own. "Molly? Molly!" she sobbed. "Oh, tell me true . . . is it really you?"

"It is, darling sister, as sure as I live and breathe. I've prayed for this moment . . . and at long last the Lord has seen fit to grant my petition!"

"And mine!" Marissa wiped away tears of happiness.

"Christmas is a time of miracles and healing . . . and this is the best Christmas gift I've ever received!"

The foursome, accompanied by Rose's children, bundled into the cutter and drove across the frozen ground to the Grant Hotel. The two sisters chattered constantly all the way and, when they arrived and the Wellinghams were ensconced in their rooms, they were still talking.

Before they went back downstairs for their Christmas fellowship around the fire, Molly deposited her packet of letters from Lizzie and Mary Katharine in Marissa's lap, knowing her sister would devour them hungrily before the night was over.

"I told Lizzie that if she ever heard from you, she was to telegraph the news to me," Molly said. "But, instead, we're going to send a telegram to Lizzie, Katie, and all our friends in Salt Creek. The news will be as welcome as it was for us to find each other!"

"That, and the news that wedding bells will be pealing again soon," Luke reminded her, lifting Molly's left hand where the glittering diamond flashed with white fire.

"There's so much we have to tell them! I want you to be my bridesmaid, Marissa!"

"And I'd love to see Lizzie, too. I have some apologies to make to her," Marissa said, dropping her head.

"Maybe if Luke and I get married on Valentine's Day, she'll have time to make travel arrangements."

"Yes, and perhaps Brad could come along . . . and Lester . . . and Harmony," Marissa added, Molly's excitement kindling her own.

"Lord willing, they'll all be here!" Molly murmured, her eyes radiating pure joy. "I can have my dress made by then. You must come to my room, Marissa, and see the fabric."

"You'll be the most beautiful bride in the state. And it'll be the town's social event of the year," Marissa said, winking at her grinning husband.

From the bottom of the stairway came a weak voice. "And I'll bake the grandest wedding cake this town has ever seen!"

Molly and Luke flew to assist Rose to a chair drawn up to the fire, where she went on with her plans. "We can have a reception right here," she said, encompassing the lobby and dining room with a sweeping gesture. "And I have a fine dress from long ago, still hangin' in my closet. Mayhap by Valentine's Day, it'll fit perfect, and I'll feel almost as comely as a bride myself!"

Molly went over to Rose and hugged her, feeling the fragile form and thinking how much younger she looked at this very moment, despite the pallor of her illness. And Molly thought she could detect the once-beautiful young woman Homer Ames had loved and coveted for his wife.

"Having a doctor arrive in town was the best medicine Rose could have received," Luke put in.

"Yes, and having Rose up and about tonight is simply one more gift on this eve of miracles," Molly added. Her eyes were shining.

"A telegram will be terribly expensive if we include all we have to say, Sis," observed Marissa.

"But a letter is far too slow. . . ."

"Don't worry about the cost, my dears," Luke interrupted. "Money should not be a concern at such a time as this."

Molly turned a radiant smile on her future bridegroom.

"Now, my darling, it has been a long day," he said, taking Molly's hand. "So I think it's time for everyone to retire, the better to rest up for the big day tomorrow, when we'll all be together again. Besides, there are still the dishes to do," he added with a sly wink.

The others made their way to their rooms as Luke led Molly toward the warm kitchen . . . where dirty dishes and precious moments of intimacy awaited them. . . . For them, the evening was just beginning.

chapter
18

Valentine's Day
Williams, Minnesota

"YOU FAIRLY TAKE a body's breath away, Molly Wheeler," said Brad Mathews, his eyes glowing with fond approval as he extended his arm to the nervous bride dressed in shimmering ivory brocade. A wisp of illusion held with a pearl-encrusted comb veiled her demure features.

"I reckon I've never felt prettier in my life," admitted Molly to the neighbor and dear friend who had come all the way from central Illinois with his wife, Lizzie, and stepchildren, Lester and Harmony Childers, to give in marriage his late best friend's daughter.

Valentine's Day, the day for lovers, had been generally agreed among the men at the lumber company to be a perfect time for timber boss Luke Masterson to take Molly Wheeler as his bride in a ceremony where they would pledge their vows before God and man.

How ironic, Molly had thought many times since her arrival in Williams months before, that she'd been intent on marrying a perfect stranger, a man selected for her by a Chicago marriage broker. Now she was about to walk down the aisle of the town's only church to stand before Pastor Edgerton and promise to love, honor, and obey that very same fellow. Only this time, her heart was filled with the knowledge that Luke Masterson was the man intended for her from the dawn of creation.

"Pa's right," Lester said, leaning down to brush a kiss across Molly's cheek. "You're a beaut! Why, you hardly look like the same Molly I used to play tag with as a tot."

She wrinkled her nose. "And you hardly look like the pesky whippersnapper who used to pull my pigtails."

"He pulled your pigtails," teased Marissa, lovely in rose velvet, "because he didn't dare yank mine!"

"Handsome as Les is," Lizzie chimed in, taking in her son's wedding finery, "I find it hard to explain why he ain't tugged on some girl's heartstrings by now."

Lester groaned. "Now . . . Ma!"

"Well," Lizzie shrugged, "I'll admit to bein' a mite prejudiced, you bein' my son and all."

"I just haven't crossed paths with the right girl yet, that's all, Ma."

"He's partial to *horses*, Liz. You know that," Brad reminded his wife.

Lizzie ignored her husband's jibe. "You've crossed paths with plenty of suitable young gals from good Christian families, Lester Childers. I expect you won't find love, young man, 'til you fairly trip over it!"

"I kinda like the bachelor life, Ma," Lester said, shrugging.

"From what Rose has said, Luke Masterson said the selfsame words," Brad reported. "There are folks in this town who considered him wed to his work until he met up with our Molly. There's still hope for you, son!"

Lester waited until the good-natured laughter had subsided. Then he took a deep breath. "Mama, I think I'm going to stay on here a spell when y'all return to Illinois."

"Lester!" Lizzie gasped, her face the picture of dismay.

"Now, Liz," Brad cautioned, laying a restraining hand on her forearm.

Lizzie swallowed hard. "Do tell, son," she croaked, stifling her objections.

"Yes, Ma, Luke and I've hit it off pretty well. He and Molly are goin' to take a wedding trip, so he'll be needing some more help at the lumber company. And after working with Seth, I know more'n just a little bit about the business. Granted, in Illinois we logged hardwoods, and this is evergreen country, but trees are trees."

"So what are your plans, son?" Lizzie asked, not sure she wanted to know.

"Luke asked me to sign on with the lumber company. I–I told him I'd think about it . . . that I'd like to."

Brad spoke up. "Then you have our blessing, son. Doesn't he, Liz?"

"Of course," she murmured, managing a smile. "'Tain't like we'll never see you again, Lester. This wasn't such an arduous trip that you can't come visit us in Illinois, or that we can't plan on another journey to these parts. Besides, there might be good reason in the near future, what with both Molly and Marissa married up after this happy day," she conjectured with a gleam in her eye.

"I'm glad you approve, Ma," Lester said, his relief evident in his broad grin. "Luke and I have a lot of plans . . . ideas that are just in the talk stage. We might want to form our own lumber company. Be our own bosses 'stead of workin' for someone else."

Brad's expression grew thoughtful. "I shouldn't be at all surprised if Seth Hyatt wouldn't be willing to buy in as a third partner to bankroll you fellas."

Lester brightened. "Luke would sure like Seth."

"And it would be so good to see Sis and Seth if they traveled to these parts on business," Molly added, feeling a pang of regret that her eldest sister would not be here on this day of all days to see her walk down the aisle.

"Seems it's been forever since I laid eyes on Katie," Marissa said with a sigh. "And of course I can't wait 'til they meet my Marc."

"They'll all cotton to him, 'Rissa," Lizzie assured. "Why, we're all plumb crazy about the man. And this town thinks he's the best thing since coal oil!"

Brad chuckled. "I've noticed, since we've been here, that Harmony listens to every word he says as if she were hearin' wisdom from one of the prophets."

Marissa, straightening Molly's veil, turned to regard the couple. "Has Harmony said anything about what she'd like to do?"

The question hung in the air.

"Why . . . no . . . I don't reckon she has," Lizzie murmured.

"Then I shouldn't be talking out of school," Marissa said. "It's best if Harmony breaks the news herself."

"What news?" Lizzie cried, alarmed.

At that moment Harmony appeared, a maturing young beauty in her Sunday best dress. "Mama . . . Pa . . . I'd planned to wait 'til after the wedding to mention this, but I suppose, since 'Rissa brought it up . . . well, I'd like to stay here, too, and live with Marissa and Dr. Wellingham." When Lizzie's shocked outcry died away, she continued. "This area needs me, Mama, and Marc is willing to train me to be his nurse, so . . . well, it would be a dream come true. Please say it's all right."

"A nurse!" Lizzie gasped.

"She can do it!" Marissa pleaded. "You said yourself that she was Miss Katie's star pupil."

"Heavens . . . a nurse!" The idea boggled Lizzie's mind.

"Maybe I inherited some of Grandma Fanchon's healing ways," Harmony said, "but I know I've always loved helping folks get well. And Dr. Wellingham could teach me the rest."

"I don't know what to say." Lizzie murmured, overwhelmed.

Brad put his arm around her. "Mama, Harmony's near grown now, so I think the decision is really hers to make."

Lizzie nodded slowly. "Your pa and I . . . well, we'd be right proud to have our own Florence Nightingale in the fam'ly, honey. And iffen you're stayin' up here with your brother, I guess that'll give Brad and me double the reason to make sure we come back to these parts regular-like."

"Oh, Mama!" Harmony cried, happy tears starring her eyes. "Thank you . . . thank you! And you, too, Pa!" she added, hugging her stepfather.

"I know the Wheeler girls and their husbands will watch over you. And your big brother will be here to guide and advise you. And if they've any human failin's in the matter, the good Lord will surely take up the slack."

Brad glanced at his ornate gold timepiece, then tucked it back into his watch pocket. "Time to put on your wrap, Molly, and make a trip to the church. You'll be goin' down the aisle as Molly Wheeler, but you'll come out as Mrs. Luke Masterson!"

Quickly the entourage departed, shivering against the cold on the deceptively bright and sunny day. Evergreen trees, still bowed low beneath their weight of fluffy snow, caught the glittering rays of sunlight and sparkled in jeweled glory.

Tears of happiness frosted Molly's eyelashes as Brad guided

the sleigh to the church where Luke and his groomsmen would complete the wedding party.

"Any doubts, darlin'?" Lizzie whispered just outside the church as she helped Molly straighten her wedding gown and adjust her veil.

Molly clutched her bouquet of evergreen boughs, decorated with tiny pine cones and tied with a large white bow. "Not a one," she murmured.

And there hadn't been, for upon Luke's return they'd spent many an evening together as he'd told her all about his rude childhood, life in the Orphan's Home, how he'd reluctantly studied the Scripture memory verses drilled into them, while his boyhood friend, now Pastor Edgerton, had soaked it all in like a sponge.

Luke had confessed to Molly that, as a youth, he had reluctantly committed his life to Christ, then upon leaving the Home, had left behind his fledgling faith, testing the ways of the world. Until Molly. But her life, her example had encouraged him to return to the faith of his tender years. Her heartbeat quickened in her breast. Now there was no doubt that he was the one man . . . the only man for her.

Poised at the rear of the church, behind the rest of the wedding party—Marissa and Harmony in their rose-red gowns, carrying sprays of evergreen; Marc and Lester, handsome in starched collars and Sunday suits, standing with Luke at the altar—Molly allowed Brad to loop her trembling arm through his. Laying his warm palm comfortingly over her hand, they began the processional down the aisle between the rows of pews.

The church was warm and homey, and it was packed with their church family members. In the back, rugged lumberjacks stood with their hats doffed in respect, their beards groomed, their countenances sober as they waited for their boss to wed the woman of his dreams.

The grin on Luke's face was matched by a radiant smile from Molly as Brad placed his best friend's daughter's hand in the grip of her intended, then turned away to join his Lizzie in a seat of honor in the first pew.

"Dearly beloved," Pastor Edgerton began. "We are gathered here today in the presence of God. . . ."

Luke's hand tightened on Molly's. Tears of joy tingled to her eyes as she listened to the most beautiful words she'd ever heard, and knew that she could fully and forthrightly promise to honor those vows from this moment forward through all the days of their lives.

"I now present to you Mr. and Mrs. Luke Masterson!" Pastor Edgerton said, beaming.

Turning to face the congregation, Molly and Luke Masterson nodded to their friends and slowly retraced their steps down the aisle, Pastor Edgerton trailing behind them.

Outside the church, well-wishers gathered long enough to bestow hasty greetings before heading for the Grant Hotel, where Rose and her girls, with Lizzie's assistance, had laid out a groaning board for the wedding guests.

"Throw your bouquet, Molly!" Marissa and Lizzie, ever the romantics, reminded her.

Molly closed her eyes, murmured a quick prayer, then sent the spray of pine boughs arching up, up into the air where a bevy of girls giggled as they anticipated its path.

"Who caught it?" Marissa cried, darting glances about the room.

"Rose Grant, that's who!" Lizzie chuckled.

Rose's cheeks grew as pink as her name. "I either had to

catch it," she complained, "or get clobbered by it, Molly Masterson!"

"You'll be next, Mama!" Becky Grant teased.

"Not unless Molly Masterson knows something I don't know!" Rose protested.

Luke gave his new wife a conspiratorial wink. "Maybe she . . . we . . . do at that."

"You'd tease an old woman," Rose accused, shaking a finger at the newlyweds.

"Old, my foot! You're always young when you're in love. There may be a second chance for you, Rose," Lizzie said, and lovingly slid her hand through the arm of Brad Mathews, her third husband, who'd relieved the loneliness of her widowhood. "You've too much love to give to remain alone for the rest of your days, Rose Grant."

"Only if the Lord wills it," Rose cautioned. "And if he doesn't, then I'm content to live out my days surrounded by those I've always loved."

"You're such a motherly type, Rose," Lizzie said, "a lot like me, I'd wager. I'd consider it a special blessin' if you'd look out for my young'uns the same as I would iffen I was here."

"Consider it a promise given," Rose agreed as she clambered onto the sled bound for the Grant Hotel.

"I don't know when I've ever been happier or more proud," Lizzie sighed as Brad tucked her into the sleigh where they were riding in a place of honor next to the newlyweds.

"I know *I* haven't been," Molly whispered, gazing adoringly at her new husband.

Luke looked down at his bride and his expression softened with love. "This is only the beginning, Molly darling. For I consider it my sacred duty to preserve that joy shining in your eyes forever and ever . . . from this day forward."